THE ORPHANS OF COYOTE CREEK

DATE DUE

DEC 1 2 1998	NOV 2 0 2016	
FEB 1 1 1999	MAR 0 1 2019	
MAY 5 1999		
MAR 3 0 2001		
JUN 2 5 2004		
MAR 1 - 2005		
APR 1 9 2007		
JUN 2 7 2009		
APR 0 8 2011		
DEC 0 3 2011		
0 5 2013		
NOV 1 2 2014		

THE ORPHANS OF COYOTE CREEK

Lewis B. Patten

Chivers Press • G.K. Hall & Co.
Bath, England   Thorndike, Maine USA

This Large Print edition is published by Chivers Press, England, and by G.K. Hall & Co., USA.

Published in 1997 in the U.K. by arrangement with Golden West Literary Agency.

Published in 1997 in the U.S. by arrangement with Golden West Literary Agency.

U.K. Hardcover ISBN 0–7451–8950–4 (Chivers Large Print)
U.K. Softcover   ISBN 0–7451–8961–X (Camden Large Print)
U.S. Softcover   ISBN 0–7838–2007–0 (Nightingale Collection Edition)

The text of this Large Print edition is unabridged.
Other aspects of the book may vary from the original edition.

Set in 16 pt. New Times Roman.

Printed in Great Britain on acid-free paper.

British Library Cataloguing in Publication Data available

Library of Congress Cataloging-in-Publication Data

Patten, Lewis B.
    The orphans of Coyote Creek / by Lewis B. Patten.
        p.   cm.
    ISBN 0–7838–2007–0 (lg. print : sc)
    1. Large type books.   I. Title.
[PS3566.A79077   1997]
813'.54—dc20   96–44970

15.16/18.95 *Ingram*
                         10-8-98
40 211

CHAPTER ONE

Len Huntzinger was, at forty-three, a defeated man who already looked a bony and gaunt sixty-five. If he shaved twice a month it was a lot. His blue Union Army shirt was stained and stiff with sweat and dust. His heavy farmer's shoes had holes in them, as did his threadbare bib overalls.

But it was in his eyes that defeat showed most. They were as dull and lifeless as the eyes of a dying animal. They stared out ahead of his team at the bleak land ahead, showing nothing, neither fear, nor hope, nor even mild despair. Only the nothingness of defeat.

He had repaired the right-rear wheel of the wagon five miles back when it began wobbling, by tightening the axle nut on the nearly stripped threads and securing it with a piece of rusty wire. He had known when he did that that it would have to be done again many times before they reached the Rockies, which were not yet even a ghostly line on the western horizon ahead.

The trouble was, he had forgotten it. Now, as the wagon followed the two-track wagon trail along the lip of a deep, dry wash, the wheel, which had been wobbling again, suddenly came off.

Had it not been for the sheer ten-foot drop

1

into the wash, it would have been a happening of minor consequence. But the wagon was too close to the edge. When the wheel came off, the wagon skidded toward the wash, teetered for an instant, and then slid in.

Dust lifted in a cloud above the level of the wash. The horses, having been pulled over helplessly, fought the confining harness and their own terror, nickering and kicking frantically.

Huntzinger and his wife, sitting on the wagon seat, were thrown to the bottom of the wash in time for the wagon to fall squarely on top of them, and both were killed instantly. Matt, the youngest, was sleeping in the wagon bed and was hurt when the weathered wagon bows collapsed beneath the wagon's weight. It was the bows that saved his life, holding the wagon's weight just enough to provide a small cubbyhole for him.

The other two children, Jason, twelve, and Charity, eight, had been sitting on the tailgate dangling their legs. They were thrown clear when the wheel came off, and they landed at the lip of the wash unhurt. They got up and stared down with shocked horror at the wreckage in the gulch.

Jason was the first to recover. He ran along the wash ahead of the team until he found a place he could jump off. Dragging his Barlow knife from his pocket as he ran, he hurried back toward the still-struggling team.

He could see that one of the horses had a broken leg. The other appeared to be unhurt. Scared, but speaking soothingly, Jason went up to him, took hold of the bridle, and quieted him.

The animal could not stand because the weight of the other horse, lying across one tug, was pulling down on him. He sat on his haunches, front legs straight, the way a dog might sit. Jason tried to release the tugs, but there was too much strain on them.

He knew his pa would give him hell for cutting the harness, but he couldn't see any other way to free the horse. He sawed at the cracked, stiff leather, and finally it parted. Jason was able to unhook the other tug. The horse stood, legs trembling. Jason unclipped the reins and led him ten or fifteen feet away.

The hurt horse continued to fight. Jason got down and crawled under the wagon. He reached his mother's body. He had never been as scared in his life as he was right now. She didn't move, and he could detect no movement in her chest. He crawled a little farther until he could see his father. His father's chest was also still.

Numb, Jason crawled back out. He stood for a moment, looking up at Charity standing on the lip of the wash. He said, 'Ma an' Pa are dead.'

Charity's face was white, her eyes wide. She made a movement with her lips, and although

3

no sound came out, Jason knew she had said, 'Matt?'

He nodded. He went around to the rear of the wagon. Its three remaining wheels, sticking up in the air, still turned lazily. He got down and tried to crawl under. He couldn't make it, but Matt suddenly began screaming, and he located him by the sound.

He knew he couldn't move the wagon unless he hitched the horse to it and pulled it over, and he knew doing that might finish Matt. He began to dig in the soft, sandy bottom of the wash directly beneath where Matt was. When he had enough of a space dug out to crawl under, he cut the canvas with his knife far enough from Matt so he wouldn't cut the boy, then tore it the rest of the way. Rotten, it tore easily.

Matt stopped screaming when he felt Jason drawing near. He wriggled out of his small cubbyhole down into the scooped-out place beneath, and Jason helped him to crawl clear. There was a deep gash in Matt's shoulder from which blood ran down his arm. It dripped off his finger onto the sand.

The sight of blood made Jason a little sick. He went around to the rear of the wagon to get something to tie up the wound. Charity had come down into the wash. Now she and Matt were huddled in each other's arms, weeping.

Jason was able to reach his ma's small trunk. He dragged it out and opened it. It didn't seem

4

right to get into Ma's clothes, but Matt needed to have his wound tied up. Jason got a white petticoat and tore enough strips from it to do the job. He went to where Matt and Charity were. Charity held Matt while Jason bandaged the arm. Blood soaked the bandage almost at once, but Jason figured it would stop.

Until now there had been something urgent for him to do. Now realization of what had happened and what its consequences might be hit him like a blow. He was twelve, and he'd been doing a man's work for a long time now, but he was still a boy and he'd depended on his pa and ma to decide everything. Now he had Charity and Matt dependent on him, and he was the one who would have to decide.

Charity wailed, 'Jason! What are we going to do about that horse?'

That gave Jason something to do. He returned to the rear of the wagon and began clawing his way through the jumble of things, looking for Pa's gun, an old Civil War musket that had been converted to take center-fire cartridges. It took him awhile, but he found it finally, along with the sack of cartridges that was tied to its trigger guard. He backed out, put a cartridge in the gun, and went to the struggling horse.

He stood with his body between the gun and his brother and sister, cocked it, and put the muzzle close to the horse's head. He pulled the trigger.

The gun kicked violently, but Jason had fired it before and was ready for it. The horse immediately went limp. Charity said, 'What if Injuns heard the shot?'

'Ain't no Injuns around here. Besides, we're down in a gully. The sound wouldn't carry very far.'

'You better look.'

'You look. I got things to do.'

She left Matt, who had stopped crying and was now knuckling his eyes. His face was streaked with tears and dust. Jason noticed with relief that the blood spot on the bandage hadn't gotten any larger.

Standing there looking at the wreckage, Jason decided there was no use trying to salvage anything except for extra clothes, some blankets, and some food. Even if he could right the wagon and repair it, he had only one horse left to pull it with. Furthermore, it would be impossible to get it out of the gully.

He burrowed into the back of the wagon, dragging out as many extra clothes as he could. Some of Charity's were in the trunk with those that had belonged to Ma. After he had gathered a little pile of clothes, he pulled out all the blankets he could find. What little flour they had left had spilled, as had the sugar. Fortunately, Ma had baked bread yesterday, and there were several loaves left. He dragged them out and put them on the top of the pile.

Charity had returned. Jason asked,

6

'See anything?'

She shook her head. Jason began tying things up so they could be carried. He tied the clothing and bread in one blanket, the remaining blankets in another one. Then he tied the two blankets together with a piece of rope so that the bundles would hang one on each side of the horse. He went to the horse and removed the harness, leaving the bridle on. He said, 'Ain't no use in staying here. We'd better get going.'

Charity looked at him in horror. 'What about Ma and Pa? Ain't we going to bury them? We can't just leave them like that!'

Jason said, 'I can't get them out. They're underneath the wagon.'

'But we can't...'

Jason said, 'I been trying to think what they'd want us to do, and I figure they'd want us to go on.'

Charity began to cry. Matt joined her. Jason stared at the two with uncertainty. He felt as bad as they did about leaving Ma and Pa this way. He knew they ought to be buried, but the responsibility for Charity and Matt was his now, and that responsibility weighed heavily on him.

Furthermore, he was scared. They were alone out here in the middle of nowhere, with only enough food to last a couple of days. Even if they safely reached a settlement, their troubles wouldn't be over by any means. They

7

still had to eat, and they had to have a place to stay. Maybe they could get by sleeping outdoors during the late spring and summer, but when fall came they'd have to have a roof over their heads.

And that wasn't the least of the things that scared him. If they called on adults for help, the first thing they'd do would be to separate them. One family would take Charity, another would take Matt, and another would take him.

Stubbornly he made up his mind that they weren't going to be separated. They were all the family any of them had now, and they were going to stay together no matter what.

Gruffly he said, 'Quit blubberin' and come on.' They didn't stop, so Jason yelled at them. 'I said quit blubberin'! Get up, and I'll help you on the horse!'

Charity stopped crying, and so did Matt. The two got up, their faces dirty and streaked with tears. They shuffled toward the horse.

Jason boosted Matt up first, then Charity. He led the horse along the wash until he found a place where he could mount. They rode along the bottom of the wash for more than a mile before they found a place where the horse could climb out.

Up on the level of the plain, Jason was more scared than before, but he didn't let it show. He took the wagon road and headed west the way they'd been going when the wagon wrecked.

He didn't let either Charity or Matt know he

8

was doing it, but he kept scanning the horizon uneasily, looking for anything that moved. He knew this was Indian country, and he'd heard stories about what Indians did to the whites they caught. He wondered if they ought to travel at night, then discarded the idea. They'd get lost if they tried traveling at night.

He thought about his pa, surprised that he didn't feel anything. He knew he ought to feel sad that Pa was dead, but he wasn't. He realized that he had mostly just felt sorry for Pa. Mixed with pity there had been impatience because Pa gave up so easily. Pa had failed in Missouri. He'd failed to keep up with the wagon train. He would never have done any better out west, either. He'd have failed out here just the same as he'd failed in Missouri.

And Ma. She'd got so used to Pa failing that she'd also given up. She'd gotten so she accepted being hungry and ragged and poor, just the way Pa had.

Jason clenched his jaws. He was going to be different. He wasn't going to give up, no matter how hard things got.

He remembered the horse he'd had to shoot. If he'd been thinking, he'd have cut some meat off the horse. Maybe it would have gone against the grain, but the time might come when surviving depended on less, and if they were going to survive, he was going to have to avoid making any more mistakes.

He opened the trapdoor of the rifle, ejecting

9

the spent cartridge. He inserted a live one and closed the action. Charity heard and turned her head, fright showing in her eyes. 'What do you see?' she whispered.

'Nothing. I was just loading the gun.'

'Where are we going, Jason?'

'Same place we was headed before. Out west.'

'Hadn't we ought to turn around and go home?'

'What's at home? They'd send us to the orphanage. We'd get split up.'

'What'll they do with us out west?'

'How do I know? We got to get there first. Then we'll worry about what they're going to do with us.'

'You're sure Ma an' Pa was dead?'

'Sure I'm sure.'

'How could you tell?'

'They wasn't breathing. That's how I could tell.'

Matt started whimpering. 'My arm hurts.'

Jason stopped the horse. He loosened the bandages on Matt's arm, but the boy didn't stop whimpering. Charity asked, 'When are we going to stop?'

'We got to go as long as we can. When it's dark we'll stop.'

He thought about it getting dark, and his chest felt cold. He thought: I'll just take me one thing at a time. He tried not to think about the

10

three of them spending the night out here all alone.

CHAPTER TWO

It was early May, and the afternoon was warm. The sky was mostly clear, but over in the west black clouds were piling high. Jason Huntzinger saw that they were coming toward him rapidly, boiling and changing shape as they did.

They looked like clouds he had seen in Missouri, out of which tornadoes came. Uneasily he watched them. At four a wind stirred, and grew stronger and colder, and half an hour later the clouds obscured the sun.

It grew steadily darker after that. Jason began looking around for shelter, but there wasn't any ahead of him. The land stretched away, nearly flat, for as far as he could see.

The wind strengthened and grew cold. Charity turned her head and looked at him with scared eyes, but she didn't say anything. Matt had stopped crying and had dozed off, kept upright by Charity's arms encircling him.

The storm struck with a fury unparalleled in Jason Huntzinger's experience. Minutes before it did, he could see it coming, like a curtain rolling across the land, but he wasn't really scared until it enveloped them, not rain as he had thought, but sleet, driven on a gale-

11

strength wind, stinging and blinding and instantly making the horse turn aside.

May. And snow. It was unbelievable, or at least would have been unbelievable in Missouri. But this was the high plain, and the storm came straight off the icy peaks of the Continental Divide.

Matt woke up, screaming with cold and fright. Charity hugged him closer, trying to shield his face with her arms. Jason fought to turn the horse back onto his original course, following the wagon road, but the horse would have none of it. He put his rump to the wind and stopped, and no sawing on the reins or kicking in the flanks would make him turn and go west again.

To Jason it seemed as if they were suspended in space, high above the earth. So thick was the driving snow that he couldn't even see the ground.

He knew they had to find shelter, and very soon. They'd freeze to death sitting here on the horse's back, exposed to the sweep of icy wind. He would have to trust the horse, he thought, and hope the animal's instinct would take him to shelter before it was too late.

He let the reins go slack and kicked his heels against the horse's sides. The animal moved ahead at a plodding walk.

The wind, now, was at Jason's back. It chilled him to the bone in minutes. He could feel the blankets beneath his knees in the bundles slung over the horse's back, but he didn't dare try to get to them, knowing he might drop them or they might be snatched out of his hands by the wind and lost in the swirling void. He also knew that if they lost the blankets they would die. They would freeze out here on this vast and empty plain, and their bodies might not be found for months.

He would just have to stand the cold. He began to shiver violently, and his teeth chattered uncontrollably. His hands turned numb, and he was afraid he would drop the reins. He alternated, sitting first on one hand, then on the other, to keep feeling in them. They began to hurt.

How long they traveled this way, Jason didn't know. An hour, two, three. Charity was silent, but Matt whimpered. Jason knew the two were protected from the wind by his body, and probably in no danger. But he also knew that he was in deadly danger of freezing, and there was nothing he could do about it, at least until the horse found shelter of some kind. If he ever did.

So suddenly that it startled him, a huge black something loomed up ahead. Jason recognized it immediately as a bluff. The horse broke into a trot. Traveling through a jumble of rocks that had broken from the rocky rim of the bluff in ages past, he went around, and then, suddenly, the air was almost still. The horse had found the lee side of the bluff.

13

The horse stopped. Jason was so cold that he doubted if he could move. He also knew he must. He slid back onto the horse's rump and tried to lift one leg over so that he could get down. The leg refused to move.

Jason reached down and got hold of it with both his hands. He lifted it, then slid off the horse. He fell when he hit the ground, and lay there for a moment, feeling warm and drowsy, wanting nothing so much as to just quietly and peacefully go to sleep.

He fought the feeling angrily, because he had heard that was the way you felt just before you froze to death. He forced himself to his hands and knees, then pulled himself up by grabbing onto the horse's leg. The animal was old and docile, and he stood quietly. Jason shouted, 'Come on, get down! Come on, Matt!'

Charity slid Matt down to him, and Jason put him on the ground. He raised his arms and caught Charity, and both of them tumbled helplessly to the ground.

Jason got up again, got hold of the bundles slung over the horse's back, and pulled them clear. He looked around.

It was not yet dark, and here, where the sleet and snow were not driven so ferociously by the wind, he was able to see for a hundred yards. He spotted a rock twice as tall as his head and knew it was probably the best shelter he would find. Matt was screaming now, so Jason yelled at Charity, 'Get him over to that rock! I'll bring

14

the horse!'

Charity pulled Matt to his feet and dragged him toward the rock. There was about two inches of combined sleet and snow on the ground. Jason got the horse's reins in his numbed hands, and with the bundles slung over his shoulder, followed them. He dropped the horse's reins on the lee side of the rock. Charity and Matt were already sitting with their backs to the rock, Charity having cleared a spot large enough for them all to sit.

Jason joined them, keeping Matt between them, where it would be warmest. He untied the blankets and one by one spread them over himself, Charity, and Matt. There were four in all.

He began to feel warmer, but he couldn't seem to stop shivering. His legs and feet were numb, and so were his arms and hands. Matt was whimpering from the pain caused by warming up after being so cold. Charity stood it in silence, as did Jason. He knew the pain was going to get worse.

And it did. As he continued to get warmer, the pain in his hands became nearly intolerable. He bit his lip and clenched his jaws, but he didn't make a sound.

Overhead, the wind howled against the rimrock of the bluff. Snow sifted down on the three children, piling up on the blankets and on the horse's back. Jason dozed off at last, and all three slept. Snow sifted down, covering them,

15

covering the ground even more deeply.

Several times during the night, Jason awoke, worried about Charity and Matt. But they were sleeping peacefully, apparently warm enough.

A couple of hours before dawn, Jason awoke again, and this time he remained awake, worrying about the awesome task facing him tomorrow. The wagon road would be covered and might not be visible again for days, if he ever managed to locate it.

The only practical thing to do, he decided, was travel west. The mountains lay to the west, and there must be roads and trails running across the prairie at their base.

The sky gradually turned gray, but Jason didn't wake Charity and Matt until the sun came up. Then he got up, shook out the blankets, and made bundles of them again. He gave Charity and Matt each a piece of bread and ate a small piece himself. He brushed the snow off the horse's back and boosted Matt and Charity up. He found a rock he could stand on to mount himself, and led the horse over next to it. He mounted and headed west, with the sky clear and the sun warm upon his back.

Behind, they left a trail, a plain, fresh trail that would remain until the snow was gone.

* * *

16

Al Gruber crossed the trail at noon. He was a tall, wiry man, dressed in parts of cast-off Union Army uniforms. His hair, which fell to his shoulders, was a light brown in which the few streaks of gray scarcely showed. His beard was untrimmed and managed to hide all of his face except for forehead, eyes, and the upper part of his cheeks, burned a mahogany brown by exposure to the sun.

His eyes were blue, narrowed today against the blinding glare of the sun on the newly fallen snow. They were as hard as bits of steel.

He rode a shaggy, diminutive horse that was as tough and durable as he was himself. When he came upon the trail, he halted and stared down at it, a light frown on his face. Even without dismounting he knew it couldn't have been made by an Indian horse, because the horse had once been shod. He also knew that it had not been made by a loose horse, because if it had, it would not have traveled so straight a line.

A white man's horse, then, with a white man riding it. Purely out of curiosity he turned his own horse and followed the plain trail in the snow.

He judged the trail to be four or five hours old. But he had no definite destination and no plans. Furthermore, following this trail in the snow offered as much promise for profit as anything. He kicked his horse into a trot so that he might overtake the rider before it got

17

dark tonight.

All afternoon he traveled, holding his shaggy mount to the same steady trot. Gradually the tracks got fresher as he closed the distance separating them. The sun grew warmer, the snow got slushy, and water ran deep and muddy in the gullies and dry streambeds that crisscrossed the plain.

It was past sundown when Gruber spotted the brown shape of the horse he had been following in a little grove of trees ahead of him. He halted immediately, amazed to see three figures in the grove near the horse. All three were busily moving around, gathering firewood.

Kids, he thought. Three kids. What in the hell were three kids doing crossing the prairie alone?

Shrugging lightly, he touched the horse's sides with his heels and rode toward them. He kept himself hidden by riding in low-lying ground, and appeared suddenly less than a hundred yards away.

They were, indeed, three kids. The oldest, a boy, looked to be about twelve. He guessed the girl might be four years younger, and the youngest, also a boy, couldn't have been much more than four.

Immediately upon glimpsing him, the boy snatched up a rifle, an old, converted musket from the war. He brought it to his shoulder and leveled it at Al Gruber. His voice came out

18

shrill and scared. 'Stay right there, mister! Who are you and what do you want?'

Gruber put on his most engaging grin, but his eyes didn't soften a bit. He drawled, 'Why, kid, old Al Gruber don't mean you no harm. Put down that thing, and we'll build us a fire and cook up some grub. I got side meat an' flour, and we'll have us a feast ready before it's dark.'

The rifle wavered a little, and so did the determination in the eyes of the boy. Gruber said, turning away, 'All right. I'll go on my way. I just figured maybe you three was short of grub, an' I figured to share with you.'

The rifle sagged. The boy let the hammer down to half-cock. He said, 'All right. I guess we could use a feed.'

Gruber slid off his horse. He unsaddled and picketed his horse to graze where the snow had been thawed by the hot daytime sun. Carrying his saddle, he walked to where the boy still stood. The boy had put the rifle down and was now trying to start a fire.

Gruber knelt and helped him out. When the fire was going good, he got a pan out of a gunnysack tied behind his saddle, along with a slab of bacon and a small sack of flour wrapped in oilcloth to keep it dry. He busied himself cutting slices from the bacon slab, and without looking at the boy, asked, 'What's your name, boy, an' what you doin' away out here all alone?'

19

'Jason Huntzinger. We're headin' west.'

'Where's your folks? Somethin' happen to 'em?'

'Wagon fell into a gulch. Ma an' Pa was killed.'

Gruber whistled. 'Whereabouts was that?' He was thinking of all the things the kids had to have left behind.

'Back about a day and a half,' Jason said.

'Followin' the wagon road, was you?'

'Yes, sir.'

Gruber abandoned the thought of going back and looting the wagon. Chances were, it had already been found. Even if it hadn't, looting it on the wagon road was too big a chance to take.

He finished slicing bacon and put it into the pan. He set it on the fire. The girl and the little boy came to the fire, drawn by the smell, and watched him silently, big eyes staring at him disconcertingly. He put his attention on his cooking. He mixed up some batter, and when the bacon was finished, dropped it into the bacon grease to fry.

He had been studying the children's horse. The animal wasn't young, but he was strong and in good shape. He hadn't a saddle, but he'd bring at least fifty dollars in the first settlement Gruber reached.

The gun was worth less, but it would probably bring eight or ten dollars if a traveler didn't happen to have one of his own.

20

The food was done. Gruber said, 'Guess you'll have to all eat out of the skillet, kids, seein' as I only got one plate. I'll help myself to a little bit, and then you kids can have the rest.'

He took a slice of bacon and a piece of the fried bread and began to eat. He watched the three children dig hungrily into what was left.

CHAPTER THREE

Gruber finished eating first. He cleaned his plate with snow. As soon as the three of them had finished eating, Jason cleaned the skillet similarly. Gruber took it from him, carried it to his saddle, and packed it and the tin plate away. He picked his saddle up and carried it to his horse. He saddled and bridled the animal, then pulled the picket pin and coiled the rope. He walked back into camp, calmly picked up Jason's rifle, and headed for his horse. Jason ran after him and grabbed at the gun. Gruber hit him on the side of the face with his open hand. There was enough force to the blow to knock Jason sprawling. Gruber went on, picked up the bridle reins of Jason's wagon horse, mounted his own animal, and started to ride away.

Jason got up and ran after him. He tried to catch the bridle of Gruber's horse, but Gruber kicked him and knocked him down again.

21

Gruber urged his horse into a trot.

Jason got up and followed, trying desperately to catch up. He had a sick, hopeless feeling in his stomach. Gruber had their rifle and their horse, and he was going away with them. And Jason had the feeling he wasn't going to be able to stop the man.

That didn't mean he wouldn't try. He ran until he could run no more. Then he sank, exhausted, to the ground. Gruber stopped his horse. There was a grin on his face, but his eyes were cold. He said, 'You kids ain't goin' to make it anyway. No use wastin' a horse an' gun. Injuns'd get 'em if I didn't.' He looked at Jason a moment more, then turned and rode away.

Jason was too out of breath to yell curses after him. But he was cursing him just the same. And he was cursing himself for being stupid enough to trust the man. He promised himself one thing. He'd never trust anyone again.

Dejectedly he got up and walked back toward camp. They were really in a fix now. No horse. No gun. Nothing to do but walk, in slushy snow three inches deep, and mud.

Both Matt and Charity were crying when he got to camp. Charity started to blame him for losing the horse and gun. Angrily he told her to shut up, and she began to cry again.

The sun was sinking behind the horizon in the west. It stained a few high clouds a brilliant orange that turned to gold, and pink, and finally gray. Jason paced back and forth restlessly, frowning and angry. If they were going to survive and stay together, he was going to have to do better than he had so far.

The thought of all the miles ahead of them frightened him. Matt was little and couldn't walk very far. He could carry Matt some, but he couldn't carry him all the way to the mountains. Furthermore, they had only a little bread, and that wouldn't last very long. The bleak certainty that they weren't going to make it came over him. Gruber had been right. They were going to die out here. They were far from the wagon road, and their bodies probably wouldn't even be found.

Charity and Matt had stopped crying and were looking at him fearfully. Suddenly he said, 'You two wait here. I'm goin' to get back our horse and gun.'

Charity said, 'How? He's on horseback and you're afoot.'

'He ain't going to ride all night. He'll camp.'

'Jason, don't go. Please don't go. I'm scared. What if you don't come back?'

'I'll come back.'

'But what if you don't? What can Matt and me do?'

Harshly Jason said, 'You won't be no worse off than you are right now.' He knew if he didn't go immediately, he wouldn't go at all. He kicked a spot clear of snow so they could

23

bed down beside the fire. It was damp, but it wasn't mud. He said, 'You and Matt go to bed when it gets dark. I'll be back as soon as I can.'

Both Charity and Matt began to wail and beg him not to go. He turned his back and walked away, following the plain trail Gruber had left in the mud and snow.

The sky turned darker, and stars began winking out. Jason knew he was lucky some snow was still on the ground. It would make trailing possible in the dark.

He didn't know if he would catch up with Gruber or not. The man might ride for several hours before he camped. But he wouldn't be expecting Jason to come after him, and that would give Jason the advantage of surprise. For whatever good that would do. He didn't have a gun, and Gruber did. He wasn't strong enough or big enough to fight the man, even with a club.

It looked hopeless, but it wasn't as hopeless as going back. He and Charity and Matt were finished if he went back.

He slogged along doggedly. His shoes were soaked, and his feet made a squishy noise inside his shoes with every step he took. It was cold now that the sun was down, and getting colder all the time. He began to trot, figuring that would help to keep him warm. It did. He began to sweat, but his feet stayed cold.

The trail was easily followed, even by starlight, and there was no danger of losing it.

He must have traveled at least four miles when he saw a tiny, bright spot of light ahead of him. A campfire, he thought, his pulse quickening. Gruber had camped. Maybe, somehow, he could recover their horse and gun.

He continued to trot until he was a quarter-mile from Gruber's camp. It was in a little grove of trees. Walking silently in the snow, he approached. Later, when a crust had frozen on top of the snow, it would be impossible to travel quietly, but now it was easy.

A hundred yards away, he stopped. Gruber had made himself a bed beside the fire. He lay there, a lumped shape in his blankets. Jason watched him for what seemed at least half an hour, and Gruber didn't move.

Jason thought that maybe he'd been seen, that maybe Gruber was just waiting for him. But he didn't see how he could have been seen, and he didn't see how Gruber could be expecting him.

He moved forward, taking each step deliberately and carefully. Still Gruber didn't move.

Jason's chest felt empty, and his belly had begun to hurt. That was fear, he knew, and he also knew it wasn't going to go away. He'd just have to do what had to be done in spite of it.

He reached the little clearing where Gruber slept. He stopped, his heart thumping wildly inside his chest. His knees were shaking so badly he had to spread his legs to keep them from knocking together.

He hesitated. Maybe he ought to leave before Gruber woke up. Gruber would kill him if he caught him here. And what good would he be to Charity and Matt if he was dead?

But he knew, even as he had these thoughts, that they were cowardly. Charity and Matt had no chance at all if he didn't get their horse back. And he'd have no chance of keeping the horse unless he got not only his own gun but Gruber's too.

Slowly, a step at a time, he approached the sleeping man. Gruber had begun to snore softly. With a man like this, Jason thought, sleep would be light. Gruber would awake at the slightest movement, the slightest noise. He'd move, when he awoke, like a wild animal, instantly, effectively, dangerously.

Jason was now less than twenty-five feet away. He could see his own single-shot rifle leaning against a clump of brush, along with Gruber's rifle. Gruber had placed his holstered revolver and belt close to his head so that he could seize it instantly if he needed it.

The horses were about fifty yards away, Gruber's picketed, Jason's haltered and tied. Suddenly one of the horses stepped on a stick, and it snapped with a sound like a pistol shot.

Jason froze. Gruber stirred, raised his head a moment, then lowered it again. Fortunately he had his back to Jason and couldn't see him. Jason stood absolutely motionless for a long time, hardly daring to breathe. Gradually Gruber's breathing became regular again and he began to snore.

Jason went on, hurrying. He didn't know how much longer he could stand this kind of suspense. Half a dozen feet short of the sleeping man, he made a little circle. He reached Gruber's head, and, hands trembling, reached for the holstered gun.

His hand closed on it. His eyes were on Gruber's face. He half-expected the man to explode into motion, to seize him. Gruber grunted softly and stirred, but Jason now had his hand on the holstered gun.

Carrying it, he headed toward the two rifles, leaning against the clump of brush.

He had done it! He had Gruber's revolver, and in another instant he'd have both rifles too. He slung the gunbelt over his shoulder and reached for the rifles.

Behind him, Gruber exploded into action. Jason whirled, terror striking his heart. Gruber was scrambling toward him, on hands and knees. But he was tangled in his own blanket, and this gave Jason another instant of time, during which he yanked the revolver out of its holster, pulled the hammer back with both thumbs, and leveled it. He screeched, 'Stop!'

Gruber stopped, less than six feet away. Jason backed carefully, a step at a time. He tested each step he took before he put down his weight, knowing if he stumbled or fell, Gruber would be on top of him before he could recover.

Gruber said, 'Kid, you're making a mistake. I was goin' to let you and them other two tykes go, but now I can't. I figured you'd just freeze or starve to death, but it looks like you got more sand than I figured you had. I got to kill you now, boy, whether I want to or not.'

Jason screeched, 'Don't you move or I'll shoot!'

Gruber took a slow step toward him. Jason fired.

The bullet missed, but it must have twitched the blanket that was still partially tangled in Gruber's legs, because Gruber stopped, poised on one foot. Jason backed another step. He knew with a sudden chill that he was never going to be able to pick up the rifles, go to the horses, untie one, and coil the picket rope of the other without being jumped and overcome.

It left but one alternative. Jason, his voice surprisingly steady under the circumstances, said, 'Lie on the ground, face-down.'

'Huh-uh, kid. You just shoot if you have to, but I ain't layin' down.'

Jason fired again. Though he didn't know it, this bullet seared Gruber's ribs, burning like an iron and bringing an instant rush of blood. The man said quickly, 'All right, all right. Don't shoot that damn thing again.' He lay down carefully on the ground, hands beneath him so that he could spring up quickly. Jason said,

'Stretch your hands out over your head.'

Gruber hesitated. Jason raised the gun slightly, aiming it. Gruber extended his hands.

Jason knew this would be the most touchy part of all. He said, 'Turn your head and face away from me.'

Gruber looked into the gaping bore of the revolver and reluctantly did as he was told.

Jason moved instantly. Raising the revolver, he took two quick steps, knelt, and brought the revolver down.

Anticipating it, Gruber had brought his arms back under him and had started to raise himself. His head turned in time to see the descending revolver. He tried to duck, but he was too late. It struck him squarely in the forehead.

He slumped back, collapsed, and lay spread-eagled on the damp ground. Jason quickly released the hammer and shoved the revolver back into its holster. He picked up the two rifles and ran to where the horses were.

He had to put the rifles down to untie his own horse and to coil the picket rope of Gruber's horse. He didn't bother with the saddle, but tied the rope through the trigger guards of both guns so that he could sling them over his horse.

He scrambled up onto his horse's back. Gruber was stirring, groaning, but he had not yet regained consciousness. Leading Gruber's horse by the coiled-up picket rope, Jason rode away. He had gone a couple of hundred yards before he heard Gruber yelling curses and threats behind.

Jason drummed anxiously on his horse's sides, forcing the old animal into a trot. He'd leave Gruber's horse tied when he took Charity and Matt and rode away. He didn't want to be responsible for the man's death, despite the fact that Gruber would have killed him without remorse. Nor did he want to be accused, later, of stealing Gruber's horse.

Suddenly, and unexpectedly, he began to laugh. All the terror, all the tension of the last twenty-four hours, was suddenly too much for him.

And besides, he had discovered that he wasn't helpless. Not by any means. He had succeeded in doing something he had thought in his heart was impossible.

He laughed until the tears ran down his cheeks. When he stopped laughing, he wondered what he had been laughing about anyway. They were still a hundred and fifty miles from any settlement. Gruber was still alive, and Gruber wouldn't take kindly to losing his guns and horse.

He ought to kill Gruber's horse right now and leave the man out here afoot, the way Gruber had meant to do them. Or he ought to take Gruber's horse along with him.

He knew he would do neither, because he didn't want to get into trouble with the law,

30

which he knew would believe a grown-up anytime instead of believing a kid. No, he'd leave Gruber's horse and just hope the man would be content to let well enough alone.

CHAPTER FOUR

Out of hearing of Gruber's shouting voice, Jason stared around him and then up at the sky. Traveling with his pa and ma, he had learned to tell direction by the stars. Now, after making sure he was headed back in the general direction of camp, he began casting back and forth in the snow, looking for the trail he had followed here. He found it quickly, and after that followed it.

He knew he didn't have much time. If Gruber hurried, he could catch up in less than an hour. Jason tried to kick his horse into a lope, but the animal refused to go faster than a trot.

Charity and Matt were huddled together near the fire, which they had kept burning while he was gone. Charity began to cry with relief when she saw him coming. Sliding down, he said, 'No time for blubberin'. Come on and get on the horse.'

'What are you going to do with his horse?'

'Leave him here. I ain't going to be accused of stealing him.'

'He'll follow.'

'Maybe not. I've got his guns.'

She didn't argue after that. Jason got the tied-together guns off Gruber's horse and slung them over his own. He made some new holes in Gruber's gunbelt and strapped the revolver around his waist, scowling fiercely at Charity as a warning to her not to laugh. She didn't. She was too scared, or maybe she was awed by what he had done.

He boosted her and Matt up. He tied Gruber's horse to a scrubby tree. Then he climbed up behind Charity and kicked the horse in the ribs, heading toward the west.

It was still dark, but there was a gray line along the horizon behind them. Gradually as they traveled, the sky grew lighter, and finally the sun came up.

Its warmth felt good on Jason's back. He glanced back often, looking for Gruber, but he didn't see him. An hour passed. Another dragged slowly by.

Jason began to look ahead more than he looked behind, because he knew what Gruber probably had done. Without a gun, Gruber didn't want to try overtaking them from behind, knowing Jason would shoot him before he'd let him catch up with them. He would, instead, try to surprise them with some kind of ambush, whatever kind the lay of the land allowed, and whatever kind had a chance, considering that he was unarmed.

Jason began avoiding dry washes, heavy brush, and groves of trees. But at last, in midmorning, he sighted the line of tall cottonwoods that marked a river flowing across the land from north to south.

Both to right and left, the trees stretched away into infinity. There was no way he could cross the river without going through the trees, brush, and uneven terrain that marked the river's course.

He lifted the revolver out of its holster. He fooled around with it long enough to figure out how to punch the empties out. When he had, he replaced them with live cartridges from the belt.

Charity kept glancing back at him uneasily. 'What you doing that for?'

Jason said, 'He ain't caught up with us, and I don't figure he's the kind that would give up. So I figure he's got to be ahead of us. He's likely to be waiting when we reach them trees.'

'Can't we go some other way?'

'Ain't no other way to go. River's got to be crossed, and there's trees in its bottom for as far as you can see.' He shoved the revolver back into its holster. He gripped the horse tightly with his knees to keep Charity from knowing how much they were trembling.

Matt was sleeping, his head lolling back against Charity. Jason asked. 'You think Matt's all right?'

She put her cheek against Matt's flushed

33

face. 'He's feverish.'

'What about his arm? You think it's festerin'?'

Cautiously she touched the bandage on Matt's arm. The boy cried out, awoke briefly, then dozed off again. Charity said. 'I think it is. What do you reckon we ought to do?'

'Ain't much we can do until we stop. And I'm scared to stop.'

'Matt's going to be all right, ain't he?'

'Sure,' he said confidently. 'Sure he is.' But he was scared for Matt. An infected, festering arm was dangerous. Still, it hadn't been very long since Matt was hurt, and it wasn't likely he was in any serious danger yet.

Worry about Matt continued to nag him, though, as they approached the line of trees that marked the river bottom. It looked to Jason like the level of the bottom was six to eight feet below the level of the surrounding plain. The river bottom was close to half a mile wide, with the narrow sandy riverbed visible twisting back and forth within the flood plain carved by the river waters when it flooded every spring. Jason rode an undeviating course, straight toward it, figuring Gruber would position himself directly ahead. When he was less than a hundred yards away, however, he turned the horse's head, drummed on his sides, and rode a parallel course to the river bottom for about a quarter-mile.

He was rewarded by seeing Gruber

galloping to intercept. Jason turned toward the bottom again, the revolver ready in his hand. He reached the edge, and looked down at Gruber's scowling, angry face.

He did not expect what happened next. Gruber spurred his horse straight toward Jason's, forcing the animal up a steep trail to the level of the plain. At the same time, Gruber raised both arms, one holding his hat, and waved them wildly. He let out a shriek that must have been as startling to Jason's horse as it was to Jason himself, because the animal shied, half-turned, and momentarily losing his footing in the mud, dumped Jason, Charity, and Matt on the muddy ground.

Gruber was off his horse instantly, running toward Jason as swiftly as he could. Jason, the gun in his hand, fought to free himself from the pile containing Charity, Matt, and himself. He could see he wasn't going to make it in time, but he brought the gun up anyway, thumbing the hammer back as he did.

Almost to him, Gruber slipped in the treacherous mud underfoot. He went down to his hands and knees. The split-second thus afforded Jason gave him time to sight the level gun and fire it.

The bullet caught Gruber in the thigh. He grunted with the shock of the bullet striking him, tried to get to his feet and failed when the leg wouldn't support his weight. He lay there in the mud, holding his leg, looking at Jason with

35

enough virulence to kill.

Jason made it to his feet, shaking so badly he could scarcely stand. Charity was crying, and so was Matt—Charity with fear, Matt with pain. Jason led the horse down into the river bottom and called Charity and Matt to follow him. He helped them both to mount. Then he climbed back up the steep bank to where Gruber was.

Charity wailed, 'Jason! You ain't going to kill him, are you? Jason, don't!'

Jason said, 'I ain't going to kill him. Now, shut up and stay put until I come back.'

Gruber tried to get to his feet, and failed again. Blood had soaked his muddy pants and had dripped into the mud beneath his leg. His hands were sticky with it. He said, 'You little son-of-a-bitch, I'm going to kill you now if it's the last thing I ever do.'

Jason didn't reply. He walked to where Gruber's lathered horse was standing. He cocked the revolver and put the muzzle against the horse's neck, just behind the jawbone.

Gruber yelled, 'Hey!' but it was too late. Jason fired, and the horse went down as if he had been sledged. He rolled over on one side and lay still.

Jason shoved the revolver back into the holster at his side. Gruber, his tone changed, now whined, 'Boy, you can't leave me here! I'll die!'

Jason hoped his voice would come out

36

steady. He said, 'You didn't have to follow us.'

'You had my guns. A man can't live without a gun.'

Jason said, 'You'd better try.' He slid down the bank to the river bottom. He led the horse to a place from which he could mount. He climbed up behind Charity.

Gruber was cursing furiously. Charity's face was white. Some of the words she'd heard before, but most of them were strange to her. Jason had heard them all. He kicked the horse in the ribs and rode toward the river.

He didn't know whether he'd done right or not. He knew he might be guilty of Gruber's death if the man wasn't able to travel far enough to get some help.

But he also knew his own survival and that of Charity and Matt had depended on stopping Gruber from following. The man had tried to kill them once. He would try again. The first time he'd done it only to get their horse and gun. Now he had a more powerful motive.

Gruber's vitriolic shouts faded before Jason had climbed the horse out of the river bottom on the other side. He did not look back, but rode steadily west.

He was hungry, and he knew Charity and Matt must be hungry too. And he was scared. The bread they had wasn't going to last very long. Only the Lord knew how far it was to the nearest settlement. Matt's face was flushed with fever, and all of them were muddy and wet and cold.

Jason raised his glance and looked at the sky. He thought, 'Lord, I reckon we need a little help.'

If he had expected it immediately, it didn't come. The horse plodded forward, and the line of trees that marked the riverbed receded and disappeared behind.

*   *   *

Gruber watched the three children disappear into the trees and brush that choked the river bottom. He shouted curses until he was out of breath. Then he stopped.

He looked down at the bullet wound in his thigh. It was still bleeding profusely, but the blood came in a steady flow, not in spurts as it would have if the bullet had severed an artery.

Characteristically, Gruber didn't blame himself or his own greed and callousness for the fix he was in. He blamed Jason and bad luck. But he didn't waste much time in blaming anything. He was in, perhaps, the worst predicament of his life. He was wounded, afoot, and unarmed, and it was at least a hundred and fifty miles to the Platte. There were Indians in the area, hunting parties if not large villages, and the Indians had no reason for liking whites.

The first thing he must do was stop the bleeding in his leg. After that, he would have to cut himself some kind of crutch. Fortunately, he still had his knife.

He took off his shirt and the upper half of his underwear. With his knife he cut the sleeves out of his underwear. He put it back on, and then his shirt.

With one underwear sleeve, he made a compress for the bullet's exit wound. He put it in place, then tied it with the other sleeve. It was almost immediately soaked with blood, but he knew that eventually the bleeding would stop. He wished he had some whiskey for the wound, but he hadn't, so that was that.

He got up painfully and hobbled toward the river bottom. He fell going down the bank, hurt his leg even more, and hit the bottom, cursing savagely. He lay still a few moments, then got up painfully and hobbled to the nearest tree.

He took out his knife and laboriously hacked off a limb. He worked slowly and patiently, despite his knowledge that Jason was getting farther and farther away with every minute that passed. When he had the limb cut to size and smoothed down, he cut another, shorter piece, and then, with the point of the knife, he made a hole in its middle large enough to admit the upper end of the crutch. He had to travel a long way on this crutch, and he wouldn't get very far if the upper end dug into his armpit.

The whole process took him at least two

hours. Finished finally, he climbed back up to where his horse lay. He didn't bother with the saddle, but he took the bridle reins, his blankets, and the saddlebags. He put the reins in one of the saddlebags, slung them and the blanket roll over his shoulder, and set out following Jason's trail.

Every step was agony, and despite his care in fashioning the crutch, he had not gone a quarter-mile before it had rubbed his armpit raw. He tore a piece off his blanket and padded it.

Slowly and patiently he hobbled along, following the plain trail left in the mud and unmelted snow by Jason's horse. Pain in his leg and pain in his armpit where the crutch still rubbed made his thoughts churn furiously, until by nightfall he was like a teased rattlesnake, ready to strike out at anything in reach.

But there wasn't anything in reach. He sank down at last when it became too dark to trail. He ate a little snow and a little dried meat from his saddlebags. He found a place that was fairly dry and spread his blankets on the ground.

For a little while he stared up at the stars. He thought with savage pleasure about what he was going to do to Jason when he caught up with him.

He slept finally, the sleep of utter exhaustion, and he didn't stir until dawn streaked the eastern sky.

He ate a little snow. Chewing some dried meat, he began again to walk, heading west, still following the trail of Jason's horse.

CHAPTER FIVE

Jason didn't stop trembling for nearly an hour after they had ridden away from Gruber and the river bottom. Several times he looked back, as if he half-expected Gruber to overtake them. Gruber's threat to kill him stayed in Jason's thoughts and kept an uncomfortable coldness in his chest.

There were moments when he wished he had killed Gruber, because he knew that until Gruber was dead he would stay afraid. But he also knew that the only way he'd ever be able to kill the man would be in defense of his life or in defense of the lives of Charity or Matt.

The best thing he could do, then, would be to put Gruber out of his mind. There was no way the man could catch up with them. Unless he found a horse, and there seemed little likelihood of that.

It had been nearly noon when they left the river. Now, as the sun traveled slowly across the sky, he began straining his eyes for a glimpse of the Rockies, somewhere ahead. He saw nothing but the afternoon pile-up of rain clouds in the west.

41

In midafternoon Matt began to whimper fitfully with pain in his shoulder. There must have been something on the wagon bow that had infected it, Jason thought. It shouldn't have festered this soon unless there had. Charity tried to comfort the little boy, but he was beyond comforting. His face was flushed, and when he opened his eyes, he looked at them both without apparent recognition.

Jason felt a growing desperation. And a growing helplessness, combined with anger at that helplessness. He was the oldest member of the family now, and responsible for the safety of them all. It was up to him to do something to help Matt. But what could he do?

In late afternoon Matt's whimpering began to get on his nerves. He said irritably, 'Can't you make him be quiet for a while?'

Charity turned her head and looked at him. He could see that Matt's whimpering was also getting on her nerves and that she was ashamed because it was. He muttered, 'Never mind. Maybe it's time we stopped anyhow.'

He began looking for a likely place to stop. Finally he spotted a bowl-shaped depression with a pool of melted snow water shining in the center. A few scrubby trees grew around its edges.

The patient old horse seemed glad to stop. Jason slid off first and lifted his arms up to catch Matt. He lowered the boy carefully to the ground. Charity slid down and pulled the blanket bundles off. She began to untie them right away so that she could make a bed for Matt, who was now shivering so badly that his teeth were chattering.

Jason took the bit out of the horse's mouth, led him off a ways, and picketed him with the rope he'd taken off Gruber's saddle. He didn't think the horse would wander off, but there was no use taking chances he didn't have to take.

He wandered around through the scrubby trees, picking up branches, sometimes breaking dead branches off the trees. There wasn't much firewood here, but there were a lot of buffalo chips lying around, and he knew they would burn, especially if he got a good fire started first with wood.

His matches were almost gone; he had only a dozen left, so he carefully shaved the wood with his knife until he had a large pile of dry shavings. To this he added tiny twigs, and later large ones, until he had a pyramid about six inches high.

Putting his back to what little wind there was, he lighted one of the matches and touched it to the pile. It flared up, and he told Charity, 'Keep adding a little wood. I'm going to gather up some chips.'

He walked away, gathering chips as he went. Each of them had black bugs under it, but he was used to that. He carried an armload back to the fire and went after a second load. Only

43

when the pile looked big enough to last all night did he stop.

Matt was sleeping now, twitching restlessly and sometimes making small noises that sounded like he was talking in his sleep. Jason looked at the bandage on his shoulder. It was too tight again, which meant that there was more swelling around the wound. He said, 'You know what I heard once?'

'What?'

'That if you put a fresh-killed liver on a wound it will draw the poison out.'

'You can't get no fresh-killed liver out here.' She looked at the horse. 'You ain't thinking of killing him?'

'Naw. But maybe it don't have to be liver. Maybe just some fresh-killed meat would do the trick.'

She thought about that, then said, 'Maybe it would, but where you going to get any fresh-killed meat?'

'We saw some jackrabbits this afternoon. Maybe if I tried I could get me one.'

Charity nodded. 'Maybe you could.'

Jason picked up the rifle he'd taken from Gruber. He didn't have any extra cartridges for it, but it was a Henry, which meant it probably had ten or twelve cartridges in it. He jacked a cartridge into the chamber and walked away from camp.

The prairie stretched away on all sides, rolling like ocean swells. The high grass rippled in the breeze, looking like waves and heightening the illusion. The sun was low in the western sky. Jason supposed there was less than a half-hour left before it set.

He walked for almost a mile without seeing anything. Reluctantly he turned back toward camp, but he took a different route going back. He hadn't seen a thing, not even a bird. The horizon was empty in all directions for as far as the eye could see.

He shuffled along dejectedly. He could tell himself he was a man and able to keep his family together and take care of them, but it wasn't true. He was only fooling himself. If he was so good, Matt wouldn't be lying back there in camp delirious and feverish. They wouldn't be out of food.

At least, he thought, it hadn't snowed again, and probably wouldn't now. The ground had dried, and the snow was gone, except for a little lying on the north sides of gullies and clumps of brush.

Suddenly, so suddenly it startled him, a rabbit jumped up immediately ahead of him. It bounded away in great long jumps.

Jason raised the gun to his shoulder, thumbing the hammer back from its half-cock position. He tightened his finger on the trigger. But he didn't fire. The rabbit was bounding up and down, and he couldn't steady his sights on it.

He knelt. He'd watched jackrabbits before,

and he knew this one would stop soon if nothing further happened to frighten him.

Sure enough, the rabbit stopped, sat down, and looked back. Jason steadied the gun. He didn't dare shoot at the rabbit's body, even though it made a bigger target, because if he hit the body with a rifle bullet there wouldn't be anything left when he went to pick it up. Instead he steadied his aim on the rabbit's head.

Even as he squeezed the trigger, he knew how foolish he was. He couldn't hit the rabbit's head with a heavy gun like this. He took time to breathe, 'Oh, Lord ... please...' and he squeezed off his shot.

The rabbit flopped, then crumpled to the ground. Jason got up and ran to him. The rabbit was dead, his head neatly taken off by the heavy bullet. Jason picked up the twitching animal and ran for camp.

Reaching it, he said, 'Get the bandage off his arm.'

While Charity did that, and while Matt cried out with the pain of having his arm touched, Jason skinned the rabbit with a few deft motions, having done this many times before. He gutted the animal with his knife, cut the carcass squarely in two, then carried the half-carcass to Matt. He made crisscross slashes in it with his knife. It was still warm and moist as he laid it over Matt's wound and tied it loosely in place with the bloody bandage.

46

He left Charity to keep an eye on Matt, returned to the fire, and spitted the remaining half of the rabbit on a stick over it. He got what was left of the bread out of the blanket in which it had been tied and put it on a clump of grass beside the fire.

The aroma of the cooking rabbit made the juices in his mouth begin to run. It improved his outlook, too. Matt dozed off to sleep, and Charity came to sit across the fire from Jason.

She said, 'Matt's arm looks awful. Do you think the rabbit will do it any good?'

'Sure it will.' He made his voice sound confident, but he didn't feel that way. He kept turning the rabbit, wanting to eat it raw, he was so hungry, but resisting it. Charity watched it cook hungrily, occasionally licking her lips.

It was dark when finally the meat was done. Jason divided it into three pieces. Charity took one piece to Matt and woke him up so that he could eat. He refused, and began to cry.

Charity returned. She kept the piece of meat, wrapping it in the cloth with a small piece of bread for Matt to eat when he felt hungry. Then she and Jason finished their portions of rabbit and the remainder of the bread. After that, both went to the little pool and drank.

The food hadn't been enough, but both of them felt stronger for having eaten it. Charity checked the bandage on Matt's arm. Then both got their blankets, lay down by the fire, and tried to sleep.

Jason stared up at the stars and wondered where Gruber was. It never occurred to him that the gunshot might have been heard, and he never saw the silent shapes that watched from the darkness several hundred yards away.

CHAPTER SIX

Walks Fast heard the gunshot, faint and distant but unmistakable. He was one of a hunting party ranging out a day's ride from the village on Coyote Creek. There were five of them, and already they had two deer.

An Indian is as curious as anybody, and a single gunshot required investigation. Walks Fast immediately turned his horse toward the sound, and the others fell in behind.

There was no chattering back and forth between them, as there would have been had they been white. They rode in single file, each perhaps twenty-five or thirty yards behind the one in front. White men, by contrast, ride abreast whenever possible and keep up a steady stream of talk.

Walks Fast was thirty-five. He had two squaws and three children. The others were younger, ranging from nineteen to twenty-five. Walks Fast was not a chief, but on this party the younger men acknowledged his leadership with unspoken accord. They were Arapahos.

The little column stayed in the low ground. When they had traveled about half a mile, Walks Fast slid from his saddle and moved forward up the side of a low knoll. As he neared the top, he dropped to hands and knees, and just short of it, he froze. He remained that way for a long time.

Finally he backed away from the crest of the knoll, got up, and came trotting back. He said, 'It is a boy, a white boy. He has just killed a rabbit.'

'Is he alone?'

'He was heading toward that little buffalo wallow with the water in it. There must be a camp.'

There was a sudden eagerness in the eyes of all. A white man's camp meant horses and guns. It meant bright cloth to take home for the women, and probably gunpowder and lead, to say nothing of all the other things—knives and trinkets and such.

Walks Fast jumped onto the back of his horse. He was armed with a short-barreled, single-shot rifle, as was one of the others. The remaining three carried sinew-backed bows in Indian-tanned leather cases to protect their sinew bowstrings from the wet, and arrows in tanned leather quivers slung over their shoulders. Walks Fast led out in the direction of the white man's camp.

A quarter-mile short of the bowl that contained the camp, Walks Fast slid off again.

49

He motioned to the youngest member of the party to tend the horses. Then, followed by the other three, he climbed the ridge that overlooked the camp.

Near the top, he dropped. He crawled the last half-dozen yards. From where he now lay, he could see the single sway-backed horse grazing at the end of a picket rope. He could see the boy that had shot the rabbit kneeling beside what appeared to be an even smaller child. And he saw a girl, older than the little one but considerably younger than the older one.

He looked at his companions with puzzlement. 'Where can the others be?' he asked. He did not want to attack the camp, only to be surprised in the act by the children's parents. He wanted horses and whatever other loot he could obtain, but he didn't want a fight with a bunch of well-armed whites.

None of them considered the possibility that the children might actually be alone. Walks Fast spoke to Hog, the second-oldest member of the party, a squat, bow-legged man of twenty-five, 'Go back to the horses. Make a circle and pick up the trail. Find out how many were with them and where they went.'

Hog nodded shortly and trotted back to where the horses were being held. Another brave, Red Stone, went with him. They leaped to their horses' backs and rode away, keeping their horses at a walk so that the sound of their hooves could not be heard by the children camped in the little bowl.

Walks Fast continued to watch. It appeared that the little boy, the one on the ground, had a wound in his shoulder, upon which the older boy was placing half the fresh-killed rabbit as a poultice. When that had been done, he spitted the remaining half-rabbit on a stick and commenced to cook it over his fire.

The sun sank out of sight in the west, and briefly the sky flamed with its dying rays. Gray crept across the land.

Hog and Red Stone returned. Hog said, 'They are alone. The trail of a single horse goes to that place, and none leaves. They are alone.'

Walks Fast nodded. 'Good. Take us to where you crossed the trail. We will leave one of our number there to alert us if others come along the trail to join the children in the camp. The rest of us will see what they have that we can use.'

Mounted, all five rode north until they crossed the trail Hog had found earlier. Here Walks Fast stationed two members of the party as insurance against being surprised. He, Hog, and Red Stone walked toward the little camp.

Walks Fast knew the boy had a gun. He knew he was able to shoot it accurately, because he had killed a rabbit at a distance of more than fifty feet. He knew, therefore, that it was necessary to take the boy by surprise if they were to accomplish this without one or

51

more of them getting shot.

Within fifty yards of the camp Walks Fast stopped. They all stood in silence for a long time, staring at the camp. The children had finished eating and had made their beds beside the fire, which now burned with a low, smokeless flame that gave off very little light.

Walks Fast squatted comfortably, and the others followed suit. Like statues they sat on their heels, watching the camp the way wolves or coyotes might. Walks Fast wanted to wait until the children had gone to sleep, but he didn't want to wait too long. There was a strong possibility that someone would be coming along behind the three children. It was inconceivable that they could be out here alone.

Walks Fast guessed they had waited an hour by the way a white man reckoned time, something he had learned before the killings at Sand Creek, when Arapahos often camped in the river bottom near a settlement the whites called Denver City. He got to his feet, and the others followed suit. With no talk, without even gestures, the three moved forward down the gentle slope toward the water-filled buffalo wallow and the children's camp.

On soft-soled moccasins they moved as silently as shadows. The horse heard them and raised his head curiously, but the wind was blowing from the horse toward them, so the animal was not alarmed by their strange, wild smell.

Walks Fast came into the camp first, but the others were less than a dozen feet behind. Silently he moved toward the boy, who slept with the rifle by his side, and with another gun, a short gun that fired many times without reloading, also within his reach. Standing directly over the boy, Walks Fast stooped and reached for the guns.

*　　*　　*

Jason Huntzinger came awake with a start. He had been so tired that he had gone to sleep almost instantly. Tonight he had not been worried about Gruber, because he had known of no way Gruber, on foot, could overtake them this soon.

But the first thing he thought when he awoke was that Gruber had, somehow, obtained a horse. He reached out and grabbed for the revolver. His hand closed on it, but it was instantly snatched away.

It was almost completely dark. The fire, burning buffalo chips, gave off a low blue flame that provided little light. But there was enough for Jason to see several shadowy figures. Besides that, his nose picked up the wild, smoky, leathery smell of the Indians.

Terror struck him. They were going to be massacred, slaughtered before they could do anything to stop it. But Jason wasn't the kind to give up easily. He was the oldest, and he was in charge. It was his responsibility to see that Charity and Matt survived.

Like a spring suddenly released, he scrambled away from the Indian that had seized his guns. He wasn't thinking; he didn't know how he would fight them. He only knew he must. And behind that determination was the confidence gained earlier by beating Gruber and recovering their horse and gun.

The first essential to a successful fight was, he knew, preventing them from getting hold of him. They were bigger and stronger, and if he was to fight successfully, he had to keep them from getting their hands on him. On hands and knees, and finally on his feet, he scrambled away into the darkness that surrounded the camp.

The Indian who had his guns lunged after him. One of the others seized Charity, and she let out a piercing screech of terror. Matt raised up, not comprehending what was going on.

Jason's thoughts screamed at him that he must have a weapon. It never even occurred to him to try to get away. He couldn't remember any rocks lying around in this shallow bowl. But as he ran, he stumbled over a dead branch of a tree that had somehow been missed when he was gathering firewood.

He seized it. It was too long, too unwieldy to make a weapon, but the Indian was less than a dozen feet away and coming at a run. Jason planted his feet and swung the branch, holding it by its upper, thinner end.

The lower part struck the Indian on one leg, and the dry branch broke. Jason dived forward for the thick end that had broken off, seized it, and before the Indian, his hands still loaded with the guns, could grab him, swung it and caught the Indian on one arm.

The Indian's hand, temporarily numbed by the blow, released Jason's rifle. Jason dropped the club and grabbed it. He sprinted away, but when he had put a dozen yards between himself and the Indian, he stopped and whirled.

He couldn't remember whether the gun had been loaded or not. He supposed it had, and he hoped desperately that he was right. He pulled the hammer back and screeched, 'You hold it right where you are or I'll blow your damn head off!'

The Indian stopped. With an awful, sinking feeling in his stomach, Jason suddenly remembered that he hadn't jacked in another cartridge after shooting the jackrabbit. He was holding an empty gun, but the Indian couldn't know he was.

Charity was still struggling with the Indian holding her, and still screeching. She must have bitten the Indian's hand, because the man let out a grunt of surprise and cuffed her, which only made her screech louder.

Matt was crying, thoroughly scared even if he didn't know what was going on. It was a standoff, but it wouldn't last, because when Jason didn't fire, the Indian was going to know he was holding an empty gun.

The brave began to advance, a careful step at a time, buckling the gunbelt around his waist as he came. Jason backed off. He had gone no more than half a dozen steps when the Indian rushed.

Jason stood his ground. He didn't dare work the lever, because there wasn't time, so he pulled the trigger, still hoping against hope that the gun would fire. It didn't even click. The brave was nearly on him, and Jason swung the gun like a club.

He was holding the barrel as he swung it, and he put every bit of his strength into the swing. It struck the man in the thigh, just below the waist, and numbed the leg instantly, so that the Indian pitched forward, falling, and crashed against Jason as he fell.

Jason released the rifle and tried to get away, but the Indian seized him. The Indian's hands were powerful. Jason struggled, without noticeable effect. The Indian got to his feet, and carrying Jason, limped back toward the fire. Jason kicked him savagely in the shins. The Indian, his voice angry but his words indistinguishable, cuffed Jason on the side of the head.

Jason kept kicking, even though the blow had made his head ring. He got a hand free and clawed the Indian's face. The Indian cuffed him again, harder than before, but Jason continued to kick, continued to try to claw the Indian's face.

The Indian released him. Instead of running, Jason whirled and attacked the man, kicking, hitting with his fists. The Indian cuffed him and knocked him down.

One thing was getting through Jason's head. If the Indians had meant to massacre them, they'd have done it. But he was mad now. He scrambled to his feet, rushed the Indian, and butted him in the belly with his head.

A grunt was driven from the Indian. Jason backed off and rushed again. This time the Indian avoided his rush. And suddenly the Indian began to laugh. He howled something in his native tongue at his companions, and they also began to laugh.

Stung and confused by their laughter, Jason stopped. He was panting raggedly and trembling, and he was soaked with sweat. His head still rang from the blows the Indian had struck. He stood there, knees shaking, drawing huge breaths of air into his starving lungs.

The Indian said something to his companions, and they left. They came back almost immediately and added wood to the fire. The wood caught, flooding the campsite with light.

The older Indian, now ignoring Jason, knelt beside Matt. With fingers that were careful and gentle, he removed the rabbit carcass from

57

Matt's shoulder wound.

When he got to his feet, his face was grave. He spoke to Jason, but Jason could understand none of his words. The Indian tried sign language, with no better success.

Jason did understand two things. Matt's wound was very bad. And the Indian was offering to help.

Jason stared at him, trying to make up his mind. He knew Matt might die if he did not get help. He knew their food was gone. And he knew that Gruber was coming and would kill them if he was able to catch up.

Still not sure he was doing the right thing, he nodded his head. One of the Indians left camp, trotting, probably to get the horses they had ridden here. Jason went to where his horse was picketed. He coiled the picket rope. By the time he got back, Charity had bundled up their blankets and what was left of their supplies. Jason boosted Matt and then Charity onto the horse. He scrambled up behind.

The Indians mounted and rode away. Wondering worriedly what was in store for them, Jason followed after them.

CHAPTER SEVEN

With every step Al Gruber took, the pain in his wounded leg increased. The crutch, even

58

though padded liberally with blanket, still made his armpit raw. And his temper, already bad enough, got worse. He was like a wounded rattlesnake, striking out repeatedly at nothing simply because he was mad, simply because he was hurt. Even without a gun, he was as dangerous as any rattlesnake, because he would strike at anything that came within his reach.

He should have killed all three of those goddamn kids, he thought, instead of just leaving them to die. If he had, he wouldn't now be in this fix. He'd still have his horse, his saddle, and his guns. Besides that, he'd have the kids' horse and rifle to sell at the first settlement he reached.

His narrowed eyes were vicious as he thought of what he'd do to the kids when he caught up with them. Because he hurt so much and because he didn't want to stop, he fixed his eyes on a ridge about a mile ahead and promised himself he'd stop for fifteen minutes only when he came to it. After that, he limped doggedly along, gritting his teeth against the pain, forcing himself on even when every nerve in his body screamed at him to stop.

Reaching the little ridge, he sank to the ground. He stared blankly at the horizons on all sides. Suddenly his eyes picked up a lift of dust about two miles away.

He crawled over behind a yucca clump, and thus concealed, studied the thin column of dust. He had watched it several minutes before he was able to pick out tiny figures at its base.

Indians, he thought. He counted five. They were traveling steadily west in almost the same direction he was traveling himself.

His first thought was one of savage satisfaction, thinking they'd overtake the kids and murder them. His second thought was that if they did, the horse Jason Huntzinger had, and the three guns, would be forever lost to him.

He lay there resting until the column had disappeared. Then he got up and hobbled down off the ridge, heading for the place he had seen the Indians. He made up his mind he wouldn't stop again until he cut the Indians' trail, and he did not, even though the pain, by the time he reached the spot, was almost unendurable.

Again he sank in exhaustion to the ground. His leg burned like fire. His head pounded and felt light enough to float away. His whole body ached with the additional strain put upon each muscle by the awkward way he had to walk to favor his wounded leg.

Lying there, he began shouting curses at the sky. It did no good, but it did relieve his nearly unendurable feeling of fury and frustration.

What drove him wild was the thought that he might be wasting his time. On horseback, the three kids were traveling twice as fast as he was, maybe three times as fast. They were steadily drawing away from him.

He was hungry now, and thirsty, even though his stomach crawled with nausea. He was weak and growing weaker with every mile. Only fury kept him going. He fought to his feet and continued west, veering away from the Indians' trail now and back to that left by Jason Huntzinger's horse.

Mile after weary mile. The sun climbed to its zenith and sank toward the horizon in the west. Rabbits jumped up ahead of him and bounded away, and he could do nothing but stare helplessly at them. Once he crossed a dry streambed and dug down in the center of it with his hands until water seeped in to fill the hole. He didn't even wait for the water to clear, but gulped it thirstily, silt and all.

Time seemed to stand still. He no longer looked around. He no longer looked occasionally at the sky. He had eyes for but one thing, the trail of Jason Huntzinger's horse. Doggedly he found it, now concentrating only on each successive step. Succeeding with one step, he would force himself to take another, and after that another still. Sometimes he fell, but he always got up and stumbled on. When it became too dark to see the trail, he simply collapsed to the ground and lay there in a pain-filled stupor until finally he went to sleep.

He didn't stir all through the night. When daylight came, he wakened and raised his head, and felt the pain and remembered where he was and what he was doing here.

His muscles screamed with pain as he fought to his hands and knees. He stayed in this position for a long, long time. Exhaustion told him to lie back down, to sleep, to forget his pursuit of the Huntzinger kids. But reason told him if he lay back down, he'd never get up again. He'd lie here and die, because the longer he remained on the ground, the less chance there would be of ever getting up.

He struggled stubbornly to his feet. He stood there swaying for several minutes. Then he took a step westward, and another, and another after that.

He lost track of time. He forgot who he was and why he was here. Wild and delirious thoughts ran through his head. Sometimes he babbled incoherently. But something kept his eyes and mind on the trail. And something kept him going, one slow and laborious step at a time.

He fell often now, and each time it was longer before he got up again. But all through the day he continued to plod westward, until, in late afternoon, he came upon the place where Jason had made camp the afternoon before.

He stopped, staring numbly at the jumble of tracks on the dusty ground. Horse tracks, many of them. Dimly his mind comprehended that these were the tracks of unshod horses. These were the same tracks he had seen yesterday. Somehow the trail of the Indians and that of Jason Huntzinger had crossed.

With a dull, vacant look upon his face, he staggered around the little campsite, studying the tracks. There were signs of a struggle that had apparently gone on for quite a while. Then there were the tracks of the unshod Indian ponies heading south, followed by the tracks of Jason Huntzinger's horse.

The boy had fought, which didn't surprise Al Gruber much, but in the end he had been overcome. The Indians hadn't killed the children, though, but had taken them prisoner. They were probably headed for their village, leading the Huntzinger horse.

Gruber found the bones of the rabbit in the dirt, and a few scraps of bread. He devoured them ravenously. He fell to his belly and drank from the water that had collected in the old buffalo wallow.

The sky turned dark, and Gruber slept again. When he awoke, he knew immediately that he would be foolish to follow the Indians. They were undoubtedly headed for a village, and he would have no chance, in his condition, against a whole village of Indians. Furthermore, if they had taken the children captive instead of killing them on the spot, it probably meant they did not intend to kill them at all.

His best bet, he realized, would be to find a white settlement. He could arouse anger and indignation by telling of the capture of the three helpless white children. He could probably inflame the whites enough to get them to organize a rescue expedition.

He himself would be fed, provided with a horse, and allowed to accompany them. That thought was sweet to him, because he knew that even if he didn't get the Huntzinger boy's horse and his own guns back, he'd get some of the Indians' horses and weapons of some kind or other. Best of all, he'd get even for what that little bastard had done to him. He'd see the three kids killed, or would at least see them after they had been killed. Gruber knew Indians well enough to know that if they were attacked by whites they'd kill their white captives instantly.

But he was a long way from any white habitation, or so he thought, and he hadn't the slightest idea which way to go.

He stood there swaying in the early-morning sunlight, and looked around for landmarks so that he could return to this place again. There were a few ridges and one low butte, but no clearly identifiable landmarks. He'd have to rely on following his own trail back to this spot.

He stumbled west, weaker than yesterday, but no less determined. Each step became a goal in itself. He stumbled across the land, taking a single step at a time, and, incredibly, the miles fell behind as the sun marched across the sky.

It was midafternoon when he struck the road. At first he did not believe it was real and thought it was the imaginings of a disordered mind. He dropped to his hands and knees, lowered his head, and peered closely at the tracks of iron-tired wheels.

Then, incredibly, he began to weep, and after that to laugh, and he rolled on the ground in a paroxysm of laughter that left him even weaker than he had been before, and soaked with sweat.

He rested there for a few minutes and then forced himself, by stages, to his feet again.

Suddenly, like a madman, he began to run along the road. It was not a run in the usual sense, being more of a crippled hobbling, using two legs and the crutch. But Gruber thought it was a run.

He continued this way until he was panting raggedly, until he was too exhausted to go on. He collapsed and lay as if he were dead for a long, long time.

Regaining consciousness, he tried to get up again. He made it as far as his hands and knees, but although he tried repeatedly, he could not again make it to his feet.

On hands and knees, with head hanging, he conjured up an image of Jason Huntzinger holding a gun on him, shooting him, killing his horse, and stealing his guns. He fed his hatred with thoughts of what he would do to the boy

65

when he caught up with him.

No longer did he think of Jason as a boy, and it wouldn't have made any difference if he had. He thought of Jason as a man. Jason had beaten him in every encounter they'd had except the first.

But he'd get even if it was the last thing he ever did. He'd see Jason lying dead, and he'd recover the guns Jason had stolen from him.

He tried again to make it to his feet, and again he failed. But he would not give up. Leaving the crutch lying in the road, he began slowly and painfully to crawl, dragging his wounded leg behind.

The coach was a big Concord, bound for Denver City, at the foot of the Rockies. It was covered with dust and mud, which did not completely conceal the yellow wheels, the gleaming side panels, or the gilt lettering: 'Overland Stage Company.'

It was drawn by a six-horse hitch. On the box, the driver handled the reins with practiced ease. Beside him rode a guard, a double-barreled ten-gauge shotgun resting negligently across his knees. Behind the coach rode a four-trooper cavalry escort, eating dust. There was treasure in the strongbox beneath the guard's feet, sixty thousand dollars in paper money consigned to the various Denver City banks.

The driver first noticed Gruber's homemade crutch lying in the road. Rather than run over it, he hauled his teams to a halt. Handing the reins to the shotgun guard, a man named Gregory Ratcliff, he climbed down and curiously picked up the crutch.

Standing there, he read the story of Gruber's travail in the dust of the road. The man had walked this far and had then fallen down. Unable to get up again, he had abandoned his crutch and crawled.

The driver, Andy Tippett, read several other things in the dust. The man had been dragging a wounded leg, which had left occasional smudges of blood on the road. And he had been pretty far gone.

Tippett stared ahead along the road. A rise a couple of hundred yards farther on hid his view of the road beyond. He climbed back up, after tossing the crude homemade crutch down at the side of the road. He took the reins from Ratcliff and slapped the horses' backs. The coach moved on. The cavalrymen, who had closed up curiously, fell behind again.

As the coach crested the little rise, Tippett saw Gruber lying face-down in the middle of the road a couple of hundred yards farther on.

Reaching the spot, he climbed down again. He rolled Gruber over onto his back. Gruber's face was covered with caked beard and dirt. It was burned dark by the sun. The man's eyes were closed, but his chest still rose and fell.

Tippett yelled at one of the passengers, a ponderous fat man named Theodoro Santistevan, to help. Santistevan climbed heavily out of the coach and helped Tippett to lift the wounded man inside. Tippett climbed back up on the box. Santistevan got into the coach.

While the passengers tried to revive Gruber, the coach rolled on, a towering cloud of dust rising behind it, hiding the shapes of the cavalrymen. Toward Coyote Creek waystation, four and a half miles down the road.

CHAPTER EIGHT

The Coyote Creek waystation sat squat and ugly on the bank of a nearly dry stream from which it got its name. Built of blocks of prairie sod and laid up like bricks, it was the same color as its surroundings and therefore blended into the landscape well. Heavy poles, freighted from the mountains, formed its ceiling joists and held up the two-foot-thick dirt roof. Smaller poles, laid closely side-by-side over the larger joists and brush, kept the dirt from filtering through onto the occupants beneath.

There were two large pole corrals out back. Both extended out into the sandy creek bed far enough to include the narrow stream of water that meandered down the middle of it.

A nearly used-up stack of dry prairie hay sat behind the stage station, having been put up by the agent and his helpers the summer before. The coach rolled in, bringing along its towering cloud of dust that rolled forward and enveloped it as soon as it pulled to a halt. Santistevan stuck his fat face out of the side window and bawled, 'Hurt man in here! Give us a hand!'

The agent, Dan Milton, opened the coach door. He and one of the troopers lifted Gruber out and carried him inside. The rest of the passengers alighted and followed, hurrying to get out of the dust. Tippett and Ratcliff climbed stiffly down. Tippett went inside. Ratcliff stayed outside, the shotgun cradled in his arms, his careful eyes watching the strongbox.

There had been two women in the coach. One was Jane Newton, single and twenty-one, heading for Denver City and a waiting schoolteaching job. The other was Harriet Plowman, whose husband had hit it rich in the mines and had sent for her. She was an ample woman with a rough-hewn face that left little doubt as to her competence.

The agent and the trooper laid Gruber down on a bench. Harriet Plowman moved forward without being asked. She straightened Gruber's leg, and with scissors she produced from her voluminous bag, began cutting away trousers, underwear, and the crude bandage from the leg.

The wound was filled with dirt and pus.

Around it the flesh had swollen and turned an angry red. She glanced up at Milton. 'I will need hot water, clean cloths, and whiskey.'

'Yes, ma'am.' Milton, a scrawny, middle-aged, dried-up man, was obviously relieved that someone had taken charge. He hurried away to get the things Mrs Plowman had requested.

Jane Newton, her face white and her eyes scared after one look at the ugly wound, turned quickly away. She asked the nearest man, who happened to be a trooper by the name of Mott, 'Is that a gunshot wound?'

'Yes, ma'am.'

'Who could have shot him? Indians?'

Mott shrugged. 'Could be, ma'am. There's a camp of Arapahos about ten, fifteen miles down this crik.'

Her face lost even more of its color. 'That close? Why, that's less than half a day's ride.'

'Yes, ma'am. But don't you worry none. There's enough men here so's the Injuns won't start anything.'

Milton brought the hot water, the whiskey, and the bandages. Mrs Plowman said, 'A couple of you hold him. When I start working on his leg, he'll probably wake up.'

Mott and Milton got hold of Gruber. Another trooper held the wounded leg. Mrs Plowman began to wash the wound with the hot water. Gruber's leg jerked. He came to and tried to raise up, but the men held him still. Mrs

70

Plowman said, 'Hold still if you want your leg taken care of. It'll only hurt worse if you keep jerking it around.'

Gruber raised his head and looked at her. 'Where am I?'

Milton answered him. 'Coyote Creek waystation. The stagecoach driver found you laying in the road.'

'How long have I been here?'

'A few minutes is all. Who shot you?'

There was a moment's silence. They didn't know it, but Gruber was collecting his wits so that his story would sound believable. Finally he said, 'Injuns. Huntin' party.' He stopped again, and then he began struggling. 'Where's my kids?'

'What kids?' That came from several of them simultaneously.

'My kids. The Injuns must've taken 'em! Goddamn it, let me up! I gotta go after 'em!'

'You ain't going noplace for a while,' said Mrs Plowman firmly. 'You ain't fit.'

Gruber continued to struggle. 'But I gotta. Them Injuns'll kill 'em sure!'

Tippett, the driver, had heard the commotion. Now he approached. 'What's the matter here?'

Mrs Plowman said, 'He says the Indians took his kids.'

'How many kids? And how old?'

Gruber said, 'Boy twelve. Girl eight. Little boy four.'

71

'Whereabouts did all this happen?'

'East of where you found me, I reckon. I was headin' west, lookin' for somebody to help. I remember hittin' the road. We ought to be able to backtrack to where the Injuns took my kids.'

'How many Injuns?'

'Five.'

Tippett said, looking at Milton, 'Must've been a huntin' party from that camp down the crik.'

Mrs Plowman finished cleansing Gruber's wound and began binding it up. She finished and stood up, the pan full of bloody water and what remained of the cloth in her hands. Milton said, 'I'll take that, ma'am. If you want to wash, come on out back.'

She followed him. Gruber sat up, putting his injured leg down gingerly. Tippett handed him the whiskey bottle, which Mrs Plowman had left behind. Gruber took a drink, made a face, then took another one. He handed the bottle back, then put his face down into his hands. He said, 'I ain't got nothin' left. Less'n I get my kids back, I ain't got nothin' left. Wife died a week ago. Now my kids. Oh, God, what am I gonna do?'

His shoulders shook, but with his face down and hidden in his hands, it was impossible for those looking on to tell that he was faking grief. When he finally looked up, his face was filled with agony. 'You gotta help me! You gotta help me save my kids. God knows what them

72

heathens will do to them!'

Andy Tippett sat down beside him on the bench. Tippett was a big man, six feet three inches tall and weighing over two hundred pounds, all of which was bone and hard muscle. He was about forty-five, and lines were beginning to appear in his face, mostly around his eyes, which were a penetrating blue. His was a homely face, but one that inspired trust. He said, 'Take it easy, man. Tell us the whole thing.'

Gruber looked away from those honest eyes. He stared down at the floor between his feet. His leg burned like fire, and the ache from it seemed to go all the way through his body. He said, 'We was comin' west. Me an' the missus an' the kids.' He stopped for a moment, wondering if the wrecked wagon would ever be found. On the chance that it might, he added, 'Wife's brother was along too. Well, I reckon it was my fault. I fixed that wheel, an' I figured it'd last awhile. Didn't. Came off whilst we was drivin' alongside a wash. Wagon fell in the wash, an' my woman an' her brother was killed in the fall. The little boy was hurt. Me an' the other two kids didn't get a scratch. I was ridin' ahead of the wagon, an' the two older kids was sittin' on the tailgate behind.

'Well, me an' the kids headed out for Denver City, ridin'. Injuns jumped us right at dawn. Shot me in the leg an' hit me on the head, I reckon, because I was out for a good long spell.

73

When I came to, the kids was gone. Tracks said the Injuns takened 'em. I thought some of tryin' to go after 'em, then I figured with my hurt leg an' all, I couldn't do no good even if I did. So I set out lookin' for some help. Praise the Lord you found me, mister. Praise the Lord for people willin' to help others when they need it. How soon you reckon we can leave?'

Tippett looked embarrassed. 'We ain't said we'll go, mister. Might be better if we went on to Denver an' got the military to go after the Injuns.'

Gruber stared at him unbelievingly. 'And leave my kids in the hands of them savages all that time?'

He turned his head and stared beseechingly at the two troopers and at Milton. Mott, one of the troopers, said, 'He's right, mister. We're supposed to be escorting that coach to Denver.'

Gruber asked, 'Why? Is somethin' special about that coach?'

Tippett shot a warning glance at the trooper, but it was too late. The man said, 'Strongbox full of specie, that's what's special about it.'

Gruber stared at the floor again. He didn't want his eyes to give him away. Finally he asked plaintively, 'Well, I reckon money is more important than three poor little kids.'

Mott said defensively, 'It ain't that, mister. But we got our orders. We're supposed to stick with that strongbox. We ain't supposed to go gallivantin' off after a bunch of Indians.'

Gruber shrugged helplessly, still looking at the floor. He didn't dare let anyone see his eyes. A strongbox full of paper money, enough to justify a cavalry escort, boggled his mind. If he could get the troopers and most of the other men here to go after the Indians, the strongbox would be virtually unguarded. And maybe, at the last minute, he could discover that his leg was too painful to permit him to ride. Or he could stay out of the thick of the fighting and hope most of the whites were killed in the scrap. And come back for the money afterward.

He said sadly, 'Reckon I can't make you go. But maybe I can get somebody to give me the loan of a horse an' gun. I'll go after them murderin' redskins myself.' He forced himself to his feet. When he tried putting his weight on his injured leg, he didn't have to fake the pain that showed in his face, nor the pallor that took all the color out of it, making it seem almost gray. He took a step toward the door, deliberately now putting all his weight on the injured leg, knowing full well what would happen when he did.

Bright lights flashed before his eyes. So intense was the pain that it literally blinded him. The room reeled, and he collapsed before Tippett, who had leaped up too late, could catch him. He crashed to the floor.

Tippett and Mott picked him up. Milton led

75

the way, and they carried him to one of the little rooms stagecoach passengers stayed in when there was a forced layover here.

Sweat had drenched Gruber's face. His eyes were closed. Blood had soaked through the bandage in a spreading stain.

Mrs Plowman came storming into the room. Angrily she said, 'What's the matter with you men? Can't you see how bad he's hurt? Seems to me if you was half the men you claim to be, you'd saddle up and go rescue those three helpless little kids.'

They stood awkwardly watching while she wiped Gruber's sweating face. She turned. 'Don't stand there gawking! Get out of here! If you can't help, at least don't get in the way!'

Tippett was first out of the room, and glad to get away. The others followed him. If they'd had tails, they would have been between their legs.

CHAPTER NINE

The stagecoach stood waiting in front of the stage station. The two hostlers, having led the tired horses away and put them into the corral and having harnessed the fresh teams, were now hooking them in place. Tippett scowled at Ratcliff, standing with a shoulder against the wall of the stage depot, shotgun cradled in his arms. He uttered a single, disgusted obscenity.

Ratcliff asked, 'What's the matter with you?'

'It's that son-of-a-bitch we picked up on the road. Claims his kids were kidnapped by Indians. Wants us to go after 'em.'

'We can't do that. We got this strongbox to worry about.'

'You think I don't know that?' Tippett's scowl deepened. Lost kids weren't his business, he told himself angrily. They were the business of the military, and he would report their seizure the minute he arrived in Denver City. Let the Army worry about the kids. If he went off trying to rescue them and if something happened to that strongbox, he'd never get another job as long as he lived. Furthermore, they didn't have enough men here to attack an Indian camp.

He looked at one of the hostlers. 'You know anything about that Arapaho village down the crik?'

'Not much. I never seen it, if that's what you mean. Talk is, there's maybe forty or fifty people there.'

'But nobody knows. Right?'

'That's right. Could be bigger than that. Or smaller.' The man went on with his work, short and stocky, soothing a horse now and then with a gentle hand or a soft, reassuring word.

The four troopers, herded out by Mrs Plowman, looked expectantly at Tippett. He spoke to Mott, their corporal, 'What about

77

you? What do you think we ought to do?'

Mott was a burly man with a sweeping moustache and grayish eyes. He said, 'If it worked and we got the kids back, we'd be heroes. If we failed, it'd be our ass. And if somethin' happened to that strongbox whilst we was gone . . . we'd just as well all drop dead.'

Tippett nodded. Milton, who had come out behind Tippett, said, 'You can't just leave 'em there. By the time you get to Denver, and by the time the Army sends out a company, them Injuns will likely be two, three hundred miles away.'

'Why? Why wouldn't they stay where they are?'

'Hell, man, they know how white people feel about their kids. They know damn well the Army will be comin' after them, an' they know what'll happen if the Army finds the kids in their village.'

'Then why would they take the kids in the first place, if there's that much risk?'

'Injuns ain't no different than us, no matter what anybody says. They love kids same as we do. Maybe more. An Injun won't lay a hand on a kid, an' that's more'n you can say for a lot of whites.'

'But what do they want with white kids?'

'Kids is kids to an Injun. At least, that's what I hear. They don't give a damn about the color of their skin.'

Jane Newton stepped from the door. The

78

warm spring sun made her raise a hand to shield her eyes. Tippett glanced at her. 'Ma'am.' His tone was neutral, simply a courteous acknowledgment at her presence. But she took it as encouragement.

'How soon are you leaving to rescue those poor children?'

Tippett said, 'We ain't, ma'am. We got passengers to take to Denver, including yourself. We got a strongbox to deliver. We'll notify Army authorities the minute we arrive. They'll handle it.'

'And what about those poor children? They'll probably be scalped.'

Tippett shook his head. 'Not likely, ma'am. Mr Milton, the station agent here, says Indians feel the same way about children that white people do. They ain't likely to be hurt.'

Jane Newton's face reddened. She said spiritedly, 'Even if they are not harmed physically, what of the spiritual harm? Those Indians are heathens, and they'll change those helpless children into heathens just like themselves.'

Tippett studied her. He and his wife had never had children of their own, but he was old enough to be her father.

She was a pretty girl, but there was a primness about the set of her mouth that perhaps explained why, at twenty-one, she was still unmarried. Tippett said, 'After that father of theirs, I don't reckon the Injuns are goin' to hurt their spiritual well-bein' much.'

'What does that mean, Mr Tippett? How can you judge the character of that poor man in there when you don't even know the man? He's hurt. He's been limping and crawling for days, trying to get help. If you were in his position, I daresay you'd not look much better than he does.'

Tippett grinned. He said, 'Whew! That's what I get for opening my mouth.'

'Well, you ought to be ashamed of yourself! That poor man has been through a lot.'

Tippett nodded. 'He has, at that. But I'd bet a month's pay, ma'am, that everything ain't just exactly the way he says it is.'

'How can you say that? What proof do you have?'

'None, ma'am. But I been mixin' with men a good many years, and I figure I know just a little bit about judgin' whether a man's what he says he is or not.' He looked at Milton. 'How did that feller strike you, anyhow?'

Milton thought about it for a moment. 'Don't look like the kind to have three kids, if that's what you mean. Looked like a drifter to me, one that wouldn't be above stealin' a horse or a poke if he thought he could get away with it.'

Jane Newton's eyes were now even more outraged than they had been before. She opened her mouth to speak, but stopped as Santistevan pushed his huge bulk out through

80

the door. She glanced at him appealingly, knowing him better than these others from riding with him in the coach. She said, 'They are accusing that poor man of all kinds of things. I think they ought to go rescue those poor children before it is too late, but they say it is none of their affair.'

Santistevan withdrew a cigar from his pocket, bit off the end, and then lighted it. He said, 'Their job is not rescuing children, ma'am, but getting this coach and its contents to its proper destination.'

Mrs Plowman, having heard part of the discussion, now came out the door. Hands on hips, she stared angrily at the men gathered in front of the stage depot. Furiously she asked, 'What kind of men are you anyway? Three children are captives of those heathen savages and you stand here talking about getting a box of money to Denver.' She switched her glance to Mott. 'You! You're a soldier, or you're supposed to be. Why do you think the Army is out here in this God-forsaken place, anyway? To escort money back and forth? Or are they here to protect the God-fearing white people from those red-skinned heathen savages?'

Mott stammered, 'Ma'am, I got my orders.'

'Orders!' she snorted. 'An excuse for cowardice, if you ask me!'

Mott's face turned a dull, brick red. His eyes smoldered, but he didn't reply. Mrs Plowman looked at Tippett. 'And you! All you're good

81

for is sitting up there driving those horses. Isn't there a spark of guts in you?'

Tippett, his own anger stirring, said, 'Ma'am, you're butting into things you don't know nothing about.'

'I know those three helpless children are captives of the Indians. I know their father is in there unconscious because he had the courage to try to go after them by himself. I think you're all a bunch of cowards, that's what I think. And I intend to see to it that the newspaper in Denver City hears all about this disgraceful episode!' She turned and went back inside, slamming the door furiously.

Jane Newton, her face very white, followed her. Tippett looked at Ratcliff and made a sickly grin. He said, 'Whew! There's a woman who says what she means!'

Ratcliff said, 'Maybe she's right, Andy. Maybe we ought to go get them kids. It wouldn't take more'n a day.'

Tippett shook his head. 'Huh-uh. There's something about this that ain't right, and if you can't smell it, I can.'

'What if she does what she says she will? What if she gives the story to the *News*? Her side of it won't look very good for us.'

'But the money will be safe. Besides, civilians ain't supposed to make war on the Indians just on their own say-so.'

Ratcliff said, 'You're splittin' hairs. You know damn well the Army would go get them kids.'

82

Tippett didn't reply, but he knew Ratcliff was right. And he was also beginning to feel guilty, as if he alone were responsible for failing to rescue the children. Still hesitating, he heard the door open. Turning his head, he saw Gruber standing in it, clinging to the doorframe for support. Gruber pushed the door open and eased himself out, still holding to the doorframe for support. Behind him, Mrs Plowman scolded him for wasting his strength.

Gruber's face was gray, his eyes pinched almost shut with pain. He licked his dry, cracked lips with a coated tongue. He croaked, 'For God's sake, won't somebody help me get my kids?'

Tippett wavered. He looked at Ratcliff and then at Mott. Both men's faces mirrored compassion and pity for the wounded man. He glanced at Santistevan.

The man was big and grossly fat, but his eyes were sharp, and in those eyes Tippett saw the same reservation he felt himself. Something here was not right, but what on earth could it be? Certainly Gruber was badly hurt. Certainly he had staggered and crawled a long way looking for help.

There was no way on earth Gruber could have known about the money shipment, no way on earth he could have set up a plan for stealing it even if he had. And if he was lying about the children, they'd find out soon enough. They could backtrack to the place he claimed the children had been taken by the Indians and verify his story before going on.

Tippett nodded reluctantly. 'All right. I guess it can't do no harm. If we leave right away, we can get close to their village before dark. We can camp and hit them at dawn and be back here by this time tomorrow. I reckon a day ain't going to make much difference.' He realized even as he spoke that he was thinking more of Mrs Plowman's threat to expose the whole thing to the *News* than he was of rescuing the children. It was his own considered opinion that the children were as well off with the Indians as they would be with Gruber.

He said, 'Ratcliff, you stay here with one of the troopers to guard the strongbox and the women. Everybody else that wants to can go.'

There was an immediate bustle of activity. The two hostlers began unhitching the fresh teams from the coach. The others hurried to the corral to catch saddle horses for themselves. Tippett tried to quiet the doubt within himself, but he could not quite manage it. The certainty that he had made a bad mistake stayed in his thoughts.

*   *   *

Gruber tried not to let his elation at Tippett's decision show on his face. He gritted his teeth and forced himself to stand straighter than before. His face was sweating copiously, and the pain in his leg was constant, but he knew he could ride if they'd let him. If they wouldn't, he'd stay here and at least get his hands on the contents of the strongbox.

But he wanted to go. He wanted to make sure Jason Huntzinger, particularly, died in the attack. He meant to kill Jason himself if the Indians didn't do it first. He looked at Tippett and asked, 'Would you saddle me a horse?'

Tippett said, 'Hell, you can't go, man. You'd never be able to stay on a horse.' But even as he spoke, he wondered how wise it would be to leave Gruber here with the strongbox and the two men guarding it.

Gruber said grimly, 'I'll stay on the horse. All you got to do is saddle him.'

Tippett nodded. 'All right. Maybe you got a right to go.' He knew he'd feel better if Gruber was where he could keep an eye on him.

Gruber watched Tippett stride away toward the corral. Maybe, he thought, he was making a mistake in going along. Revenge against that damned kid wasn't as important as getting his hands on all that cash. If he did go along and participate in the attack on the Indian village, he'd have to kill Jason and get away quick, before the others realized he had gone. He'd have to get back here in time to get the money and get away with a fresh horse and at least an hour's start.

He hesitated, but only briefly, wanting the money but wanting Jason Huntzinger even more. Suddenly an inspiration struck him. He could kill Jason, but he could let the other two children live. He could seize one of them as hostage, and using the hostage as shield, get away and return here for the money.

Impatiently he put all his vague planning out of his mind. He'd have to take things the way they came, altering his plans to meet changing circumstances. The battle between the whites and the Indians might even leave both sides badly mauled.

At the very least he would see that Jason died. He would get enough loot from the Indian village to more than make up for what he'd lost. And if everything turned out exactly right, he'd have the specie in the strongbox as well.

The prospect of getting even with Jason Huntzinger soon put new strength into him. He waited impatiently for Tippett to bring him a horse.

CHAPTER TEN

Tippett saddled the only horse left in the corral, a swaybacked beast of considerable age. Gruber eyed the animal sourly when Tippett led him to the front door of the stage depot, but he let Tippett boost him onto the horse's back, clenching his jaws fiercely to keep from crying out. He discovered he could quiet the pain by thinking about what he meant to do to Jason Huntzinger for shooting him. He sat there gripping the saddle horn, sweating, waiting until everyone else would be ready to go.

All but the two Tippett had designated to stay with the strongbox elected to go, even though some of them had to ride the horses unhitched from the stagecoach a few moments before. There weren't enough saddles to go around, so several of the men rode bareback. Tippett slung two good-sized gunnysacks behind his saddle that contained food and cooking utensils. All of the men were heavily armed, most with both rifles and revolvers. Two carried double-barreled shotguns. Gruber had a rifle lent him by Milton, the station agent, and a revolver lent him by Ratcliff, the shotgun guard.

Ratcliff and the trooper assigned to stay with him to guard the strongbox stood in front of the stage depot, along with the two women, and watched them ride away. Tippett took the lead.

There were nine of them in all, three troopers, Milton and his two hostlers, Santistevan, Tippett, and Gruber himself. Enough, thought Gruber, to take on any Indian village up to about fifty inhabitants.

But his wound didn't give him much time to think. He continued to cling to the saddle horn, because he could not stand the pain of putting the foot of his wounded leg into the stirrup.

For a while Tippett held the horses to a walk. They reached the place where the coach had stopped to pick him up. They went on, and Gruber saw the crutch lying at the side of the road. About a mile beyond, they came to the place where he had entered the road. Here Tippett turned east.

Now Tippett kicked his horse into a trot, and the others followed suit. Gruber's face instantly turned white, and sweat sprang from every pore. He glared at Tippett's back, sure the stagecoach driver had picked up the gait deliberately to hurt him as much as possible. He gritted his teeth until his jaws ached. He put his thoughts on Jason Huntzinger, who had caused him all this pain. He stared venomously at Tippett's back, promising himself that before this was through, he would put a bullet into it.

Only nurturing this kind of venomous hatred made his ordeal endurable. The minutes seemed like hours; the hours seemed like days. Gruber lost all track of time.

Once Santistevan rode up beside him during one of their brief halts to rest the horses and handed him a brown bottle. Gruber pulled the cork with his teeth, took a long drink, followed it immediately by another, before Santistevan could take the bottle back.

He choked and began to cough, and this made the pain in his leg even more unbearable. He stared down at the bandage, bright with fresh blood that had soaked through the old. He looked at Tippett. 'Do you got to keep these goddamn horses at a trot?' he snarled.

Tippett studied him, hostility and distrust in his eyes. 'It's the easiest gait on them,' he said.

Santistevan said, 'You're killin' Gruber, man. Can't we walk them awhile and then lope awhile?'

Tippett shrugged. He kicked his horse into motion. He rode at a walk for about a mile, then picked up the gait to a lope for another half-mile. Afterward he dropped back to a walk again. Gruber began to breathe a little easier. Anything was better than a jolting trot.

They reached the place where the Indians had taken the children. Tippett raised a hand to halt the column. He dismounted and handed the reins of his horse to one of the troopers.

Cautioning the others to remain where they were, he walked slowly forward, studying the ground carefully as he did. Gruber wished he could see Tippett's face. He didn't know how good a tracker Tippett was, but the driver seemed competent in everything he did, and the chances were good he could read tracks as well as he did everything else.

Once Tippett turned and glanced at him, a light frown on his face. He was studying the marks of the scuffle now, Gruber realized, his own tracks, and the tracks of the Indians. Tippett walked away from the spot for a couple of hundred yards, following the Indians' trail. Then he came walking slowly back. He came to Gruber and scowled up at him. 'You're a liar, Gruber. Suppose you tell us the truth.'

'I did tell you the truth.'

Santistevan broke in, 'How can you tell he's lying, Tippett?'

'Them kids went willingly with the Indians. They wasn't taken by force.'

Gruber said harshly, 'That's crazy! Why would they go willingly?'

Tippett ignored him. 'Besides that,' he said, 'you wasn't with the kids when they was took. You was trailing 'em, an' you reached here after they was gone.'

Gruber's mind raced. If this group gave up the pursuit now, they'd return to the stage depot, and the stage would go on to Denver with the strongbox. He might be allowed to ride along, but any chance of getting his hands on it would be gone. He was no match for all these men.

With seeming reluctance he said, 'All right. I guess I'd ought to tell you the truth. That kid, Jason, he's a bad un for sure. He's been in trouble ever since he was four years old. He shot me, his own pa, because I blamed him for causin' the wagon wreck. He took them two younger kids an' run away, takin' the only

90

horse we had. The little one was hurt some in the wreck, an' maybe the wound was bad enough so's they all went with the Indians to get it tooken care of.'

Tippett was still studying him suspiciously. Gruber cinched it, he thought, by saying, 'I don't care what happens to Jason, because I reckon there ain't no hope for him. But them two younger kids is damn good kids. Besides that, it don't matter whether you believe me or not. Them poor kids is in the hands of a bunch of heathen savages, and you know what that Mrs Plowman said she'd do if you didn't get 'em back.'

Tippett stared at him a moment more. Santistevan said, 'That part's right, even if the rest of it ain't. The kids are captives of a bunch of heathen savages. If we don't get 'em now, the Army's goin' to have to send out a whole company after 'em.'

Tippett nodded reluctantly. 'I suppose you're right.' He took the reins of his horse from the trooper and mounted him. Again, traveling deliberately at a trot, he rode away, following the Indians' trail. Gruber gritted his teeth and followed silently.

Tippett appeared to know the country, although Gruber supposed he might just be making good use of his eyes. It was known that the Indian camp was on Coyote Creek, the same thin stream that ran past the stage depot a dozen or so miles upstream. Tippett could probably see in the distance the winding, timbered, low-lying area that was the bed of the stream.

A couple of miles short of it, Tippett halted them in a shallow depression where they and their horses would be hidden from any lookouts the Indians might have stationed on the hills. He dismounted and said, 'All right, make yourselves comfortable, but don't build any fires. I'm going to see what we're getting into.'

He walked away. Santistevan and one of the troopers helped Gruber down from his horse. He collapsed immediately onto the ground, lay back, and closed his eyes. His leg throbbed steadily at first, but gradually the pain lessened, and after a while he slept.

*   *   *

Tippett moved quietly for so big a man, even though there was, as yet, no need for it. He stayed in the shallow draws as he walked toward the Indian village, his eyes always roving, always studying the land on all sides of him.

He wasn't at all sure that what they were doing was right, but he knew that if they didn't rescue the three children the Army would, and that would be worse, both for the children and the Indians. If it was done now with nine men it would be better than doing it later with the forty or fifty the Army would be sure to use. Chivington's massacre of the Cheyenne village on Sand Creek was fresh in Tippett's memory, and he hated to think of something like that happening again.

Adding to his reluctance to attack the Indian village was the fact that he didn't trust Gruber. He didn't like him, either. Gruber looked to him like the kind of man who would slit his best friend's throat for a dollar. If he had any friends, which Tippett doubted.

He didn't believe Gruber's story, even the latest one. And he couldn't help feeling uneasy about that strongbox back there at the stage depot, with only two men guarding it.

He walked steadily for about half an hour before he reached the bed of Coyote Creek half a mile above the site of the village. He eased along through the trees toward it and finally got a glimpse of it.

It lay on the south side of the creek bed and contained seventeen lodges. Seventeen lodges added up to no more than sixty people. There probably were not more than ten or twelve mature men young enough to fight.

He studied the place for a long time, without catching a glimpse of any white children, although he admitted the possibility that they were, by now, clad in Indian clothes. Or they might not have the freedom to come and go as they pleased, despite the fact that they had accompanied the Indians willingly.

The signs of a struggle back where the Indians had first encountered them puzzled Tippett, but he finally decided that a white boy of twelve, as mature as this one probably was, would have put up a fight before letting himself, his brother, and his sister be taken prisoner. Perhaps he'd fought so hard he had earned the Indians' respect. They might even have given him a choice of remaining or going along with them.

That reasoning seemed logical. Carefully he withdrew, and when he was out of sight of the village, he hurried back toward the depression where he had left the other men.

Gruber had said the youngest boy was hurt. If that was so, why was the older boy so anxious to go with the Indians, whom he naturally would fear, when he could simply remain and let Gruber, his pa, catch up with him and tend the younger boy?

The answer to that was very obvious. Gruber's latest story also was a lie. He probably wasn't the children's father at all. He might even have been responsible for the deaths of their parents, and he might have received his leg wound in that fight.

Tippett shrugged. They'd know the truth soon enough. When they had rescued the three children, they would get the truth from them.

The sun was low in the western sky when he reached the spot where he had left the other men. Gruber was lying on the ground, apparently asleep. Santistevan asked, 'How many?'

'Seventeen lodges. That adds up to maybe sixty Indians, but only ten or twelve of that number could be fighting men. And unless they've been getting guns someplace, I doubt if there's more'n half a dozen guns among 'em. Most of those are likely old muzzle-loading relics.'

'Are we going to hit 'em, then?'

Tippett nodded reluctantly. 'I don't see any other way out of it. One or two men would be committing suicide going in alone to ask 'em to release the kids. And if all of us ride in, they're sure to begin shooting at us.'

'You going to wait for morning, then?'

Tippett nodded. 'If we can hit 'em right at dawn, we'll catch half of 'em asleep. Maybe we can get the kids without killing a lot of Indians.'

Gruber sat up on the ground. 'I don't see why the hell we have to wait. My goddamn leg's killin' me, and you know what layin' out here in the cold all night will do to it. I say let's hit 'em now and get it over with. Besides, I'm worried about my kids, and I want 'em back.'

Gruber watched Tippett's face carefully as he spoke. He could see in the big stage driver reluctance to attack the Indian camp at all.

Gruber wanted to attack tonight for another reason beyond his own comfort. He wanted the attack to take place in darkness, or just before

95

darkness came. He wanted to kill Jason Huntzinger even if he didn't get the other kids, and he could hardly do that in daylight and get away with it. In darkness, who could say that it wasn't an Indian bullet that had struck the boy?

Besides, Gruber wanted to return to the stage depot in the dark. From out in the darkness he could pick off Ratcliff and the trooper easily. He could bust open the strongbox, stuff the specie into a pair of saddlebags, and be ten miles away by the time the attack party got back to the stage depot with the kids. He'd have all night to put more distance between them and himself, because they sure as hell couldn't trail him in the dark.

One of the three troopers spoke up. 'We say let's hit 'em tonight and get it over with. If anything was to happen to that strongbox while we're out here chasing Indians, we'd just as well plan on spending the rest of our lives in the damn stockade.'

Tippett hesitated, then finally nodded reluctantly. 'All right. Soon's the sun's clear down, we'll go.' And Gruber heaved a long, silent sigh of relief.

96

CHAPTER ELEVEN

Now that the decision had been made, the men waited nervously for the sun to drop out of sight in the west. The horses fidgeted. Tippett paced back and forth, uncertainty still showing on his face. He wasn't sure his decision had been right, but it had been made, and now he'd have to live with it.

With almost maddening slowness the sun sank out of sight. As soon as it had, Tippett said, 'Let's go,' and helped Santistevan boost Gruber onto his horse. When he saw Gruber's pallor and the sweat on his forehead, he asked, 'Want to stay here? Ain't no need for you to come along.'

'They're my kids, Mr Tippett. I'll go along.'

Tippett stared at him. They are like hell, he thought, but he had no proof, and besides, by now, he wanted to see what Gruber was really up to. He rode out by the same route he had walked toward the Indian village earlier, staying in the low ground. Before they had gone half the distance to Coyote Creek, the glow of the sun had faded from the clouds and the sky was wholly gray. Tippett picked up the pace slightly, not wanting it to be completely black when the attack began.

They crossed the creek, climbed the cutbank on the far side, and circled the low hill that lay to the Indian village's rear. The nine men topped this rise finally and stared down at the little Indian village sitting so peacefully beside the stream. There was still enough light to see.

Smoke rose from the conical tepees. A dog barked; an infant cried. A squaw scolded someone, perhaps her husband, and metal clanged against metal with a bell-like sound.

Tippett said, 'A lot of shootin' in the air ought to do it, unless they open up on us. I don't want nobody killin' squaws or kids, no matter what. You got that clear?'

Nobody answered him, but then, he hadn't expected them to. He touched his horse's sides with his heels, then dug them in. The horse jumped and went down the gentle rise at a lope.

The other men swept along behind, spreading to right and left so that they formed a line and thus would not be hitting each other with bullets aimed at the Indians.

Half a mile downstream, Tippett glimpsed the horse herd and several tiny figures tending it. He returned his attention to the village ahead just as they were seen, just as a shrill woman's scream split the air.

Men, children, and women ran from the tepees. Some had weapons, but most did not. A gun flashed in the village, the bullet apparently hitting nothing. But it was all the signal the whites needed. To Tippett's right and left, guns flashed, and the reports were a harsh violence in this peaceful place.

Tippett's own gun had not been fired. He swept his glance over the milling Indians, looking for the three white kids. A woman screeched as she was hit and went down, and Tippett bawled, 'Damnit, I said no shootin' squaws!'

He might as well have saved his breath. If any of the men heard him, they gave no sign of it. Other Indians went down, Indians of both sexes, and suddenly the milling stopped and the Indians turned to flee. A few braves stayed, the ones with guns, standing and firing, and when their muzzle-loading rifles were empty, they threw them down and followed the others to form a protective shield behind.

Tippett felt a little sick at his stomach. This was exactly what he had not wanted to happen. He had been a fool, he supposed, to think that excitement wouldn't take over and control the things the eight men with him did.

He raised his voice and bawled, 'Jason! Jason! All three of you stay down till this is over with!'

He hauled his horse to a halt short of the first tepee. The others galloped past. He bawled, 'That's enough! Let'em go!' But again he might as well have saved his breath. They were hunters now, and the excitement of the hunt was strong in them. As if these Indians were animals.

Tippett got down from his horse and started going through the tepees, one by one. His gun

99

was ready in his hand. He didn't want to shoot anyone, but he knew he'd have to if he encountered an Indian that was still alive.

*   *   *

Jason Huntzinger was sitting cross-legged beside the fire inside the tepee of the family taking care of the three of them when the first squaw's cry split the air. Before he could get up, a rifle barked, and immediately following that, a veritable crackle of rifle shots broke out on the slope behind the village.

The squaw, whose name was Beaver Woman, immediately rushed for the tepee flap and burst outside. Jason hesitated an instant, not knowing whether he should flee or stay. He didn't know who the attackers were, whether Indian or white.

A bullet tore through the tepee covering, ripped into the fire, and scattered live coals all over the tepee floor. That decided him. To Charity he said, 'Come on.' He grabbed his rifle in one hand, little Matt's unwounded arm in the other, and literally dragged the boy through the tepee flap. The village medicine man had doctored Matt's arm with poultices and chanting, and the swelling and much of the pain had gone out of it.

Charity was running as fast as she could go. Jason, dragging Matt, now screaming with terror, rushed after her. Beside him an Indian woman went to her knees, then slowly fell forward onto her face.

It was now almost completely dark. They were in the creek bottom among the scrubby trees, where the horsemen could not follow easily. Bullets cut through the branches of the trees. Jason heard Tippett's bellow and heard his name called, and once more he hesitated, not knowing whether he should go on or stop.

Finally, out of breath, he stopped. Charity had also stopped, and now stood with her head hanging, panting raggedly. Matt had no breath left for cries of fear, but he was whimpering like a hurt animal. Jason knelt and put his arms around the little boy and held him close. He said, 'It's all right, Matt. It's all right now.'

His holding the boy probably had more effect than his words. Matt quieted. Charity asked, 'What you reckon we ought to do?'

Jason said, 'That wasn't Gruber yelling, but nobody couldn't have knowed our names unless Gruber told 'em.'

'Maybe we'd ought to go with the Indians.'

Jason considered that, saying finally, 'I don't reckon they'll have us now. Look at all the trouble we brought down on 'em.'

'Then maybe we'd ought to go on back.'

Jason considered that for a moment. Finally he said, 'All right. But if you see anybody coming, yell out so's they won't think we're Indians.'

They started back toward the village. The

shooting had diminished as the Indians lost themselves in darkness or crouched down in heavy brush and grass to hide, but there was still some yelling back and forth among the whites.

Jason climbed the cutbank first, then turned and reached down a hand to pull Matt up. Charity boosted him from behind, and Jason got him out on level ground without hurting his arm. He turned and helped Charity, then faced toward the village and stood up.

He found himself face-to-face with Gruber, but he saw Gruber a split-second before Gruber saw him. Instantly he shoved his rifle toward Gruber and pulled the hammer back. The click of it was loud, and Gruber froze with his gun still pointing at the ground. Jason said, 'Drop it or I'll shoot you in the other leg.'

Behind Gruber, flames licked up from one of the tepees that had been pulled over by the whites. They cast a flickering light on Jason's scared, determined face. Gruber said, 'You ain't going to shoot.'

'The hell I ain't!' Jason shrilled. 'I did before, didn't I?'

Gruber took a limping step toward him, without making any attempt to raise his gun.

Jason knew he was either going to have to shoot or let Gruber grab him when he got close enough. He tightened his finger on the trigger; then, remembering the voice that had called out to him, he yelled, 'Hey! Here I am! You come get me before I shoot this damn horse thief!'

Behind Gruber he saw a man approaching. The man was big, with broad shoulders and tawny hair. Jason yelled, 'This Gruber stole our horse an' gun an' left us out on the prairie to die. He's tryin' to kill me now because I caught up an' shot him an' took back our horse!'

The heavyset man growled, 'How about it, Gruber? I thought you said they was your kids.'

Others were now approaching from all sides. The shooting had stopped.

Gruber stood there on his good leg, hesitating for several moments. Behind him Tippett said, 'Drop it, Gruber. Drop it before I put a bullet in your back.'

Gruber whined, without turning his head, 'You ain't goin' to believe this kid instead of me, are you? I told you he was a bad un.'

Tippett switched his glance to Charity. 'How about it, girl? Is this man your pa?'

'No, he ain't. It's like Jason says. He stole our horse an' gun. Jason got 'em back an' shot him when he come after us again.'

Tippett said, 'I ain't goin' to tell you again, Gruber. Drop that gun.'

Gruber suddenly plunged ahead. He struck Jason with his body and knocked him down. Jason's gun discharged, but by then it was pointed up at the sky. Gruber, falling, grabbed for Jason and missed as Jason squirmed away. Tippett roared, 'Hold it! I'll kill you, damnit!' But Gruber didn't stop. Failing to get his hands on Jason, he crawled forward and seized Charity, yanking her away from Matt and bringing her around in front of him. He yelled, 'Drop it, Tippett! All of you, drop your guns!'

Tippett said, 'Let her go.'

Gruber shook his head. Jason wondered if any of the men would take a chance on trying to shoot Gruber while he held Charity as a shield. He hoped they would not, because there wasn't enough light to see a rifle's sights. Finally Tippett asked, 'All right, what do you want?'

'A good horse. An hour's start.'

Tippett looked at Jason. 'What else did he do, boy? Did he kill your folks?'

Jason shook his head. 'No, sir. They was killed when the wagon fell in a wash.'

Tippett hesitated a moment. 'All right. You got my word. Now, let the girl go.'

'Oh, no. I ain't lettin' her go. If I do, you'll cut me to pieces.'

'All right, then. Let her go when you get out of sight of here.'

Gruber nodded. 'All right. Now, bring me a horse. I want the best you got.' Carefully shielding himself with Charity's body, he got painfully to his feet.

Tippett looked at one of the hostlers. 'Get him a horse.'

104

Gruber said, 'The best. I want that bay with the blazed face.'

The trooper said, 'You can't have that one. It belongs to the Army.'

'I don't give a damn who it belongs to. That's the one I want.' Gruber tightened his forearm around Charity's throat. She choked, and her face turned red.

Tippett said, 'Give it to him, trooper.'

The trooper brought Gruber the horse. Gruber took the reins and limped backward into the darkness, leading the horse.

Jason knew he'd never let Charity go. Tippett might believe he would, but he knew better. Suddenly he lunged at Gruber, about half a dozen yards away. Gruber tried to bring the gun to bear on him, but Jason was too quick.

Unable to bring the gun to bear, Gruber struck out blindly with it, staggering away as he did. Its barrel struck Jason on the forehead with a solid crack. Lights flashed, and there was a brassy taste in Jason's mouth. Then everything went black.

As Jason struck Gruber, Tippett raised his rifle, ready to get a shot if Gruber should drop the girl. But the man did not. He only staggered away a few steps after he had clipped Jason with the receiver of his gun. He recovered, controlled the frightened horse, and continued to back away. Charity was still choking, since he was holding her with his forearm against her throat. His gun was in his other hand, along with the horse's reins.

Tippett said, 'We're letting you go, Gruber, but if you don't release that girl, we're coming after you.' Even as he said it, he knew it was an idle threat. Gruber had the best horse, and no other animal they had could overtake him once he got clear.

But he didn't dare risk trying to shoot Gruber. In this kind of light there was too much chance of hitting the little girl.

Gruber backed until he had completely disappeared. He apparently changed his grip on Charity, releasing her throat, because she began to cough. After several moments Tippett heard the hooves of Gruber's commandeered mount as the animal loped away.

He swung to his own horse and said, 'Let's go. One of you hand that boy up to me. Another of you take the little one.'

The trooper whose horse Gruber had commandeered asked, 'What about me? What am I supposed to ride?'

'The horse Gruber rode here, I suppose.' At a trot, Tippett rode in the direction Gruber had gone, with Jason propped up in the saddle in front of him. The others came along behind.

CHAPTER TWELVE

Jason came to sicker than he had ever been before. His head pounded mercilessly with every movement of the horse. Tippett felt him stir and asked, 'Head ache?'

'Yes, sir,' Jason groaned. 'What happened?'

'You tried to keep Gruber from takin' your sister. He hit you a lick with his gun.'

'What about Charity? Where ...?'

Tippett's voice was apologetic. 'He took her, son. There wasn't nothin' we could do. We didn't dare shoot in that kind of light for fear of hitting her.'

Jason felt even sicker when he heard that. He swayed, and would have fallen from the saddle except that Tippett was holding him. Tippett asked, 'You want to stop awhile? You figure you can't go on?'

'I'll go on.' Jason spoke through clenched teeth.

Ignoring that, Tippett pulled his horse to a halt. To the others he said, 'Gruber ain't left her off, or we'd have found her. We sure as hell can't trail him in the dark, so we'd just as well camp here. Maybe by morning this boy'll feel better.'

Jason said stubbornly, 'Don't you be worryin' about me. I can go on.'

'No use, son. We can't read trail.' Steadying

107

Jason, he dismounted, then eased Jason down. Tippett spoke to the men, 'Build a fire if you can find some chips. I got grub in these here gunnysacks.'

He took care of his horse, unsaddled and picketed him some distance away from camp. He returned and dug provisions and utensils out of the gunnysacks. He hunkered down a few feet from Jason and looked at him. 'You go with them Injuns of your own free will, or did they take you?'

'We just went with them. Matt's arm was festerin' an' I was scared he was goin' to get worse.'

'Injuns treat you right?'

'Yes, sir. They treated us just like we was theirs.'

Tippett said, 'I'm sorry, boy. I'm sorry we paid 'em back like we did. I just figured there wasn't no way to get you kids away from 'em short of shootin' the village up. Besides that, we figured if they knew we knew you was there, they'd get rid of you, an' we didn't want that happening.'

Tippett watched as someone kindled a fire with buffalo chips, feeding more fuel as the fire grew. After a while he asked, 'How's the head? Any better?'

'Yes, sir. It's better when I ain't moving it.'

'What really happened to your ma an' pa?'

'Wagon wheel came off. Wagon slid into a wash an' pinned Ma an' Pa underneath. We

108

had to leave 'em there because we couldn't get to 'em. You reckon that was all right? I know I ought to've buried 'em, but I couldn't get to them.'

Tippett said, 'We'll send somebody out to recover the bodies, son. Was they on a regular wagon road?'

'Yes, sir.'

'Then likely somebody's already taken care of them. Don't fret about it.' He studied the boy for a while in the firelight. Jason was tall for a boy of twelve, but he had grown upward at the expense of his outward growth. He was thin and stringy, but what he lacked in heft he more than made up in courage, Tippett thought.

He and his wife had never had children, and he'd never known whether that was his doing or hers. He thought now that if he'd had a boy, he'd have wanted one with Jason's fortitude. He asked, 'What you going to do after we get your sister back?'

'Go on, I reckon.'

'Where you headed for?'

'The goldfields.'

'Colorado or California?'

'Colorado. Pa never done much good at farmin'. He figured maybe he'd do better in the mines. He figured if he didn't strike it rich, he'd at least have a steady job.'

'You figure you can support the three of you?'

109

'I reckon so.' There was a world of calm assurance in Jason's voice.

'Some of them Denver busybodies get hold of you and they'll...' Tippett stopped. He didn't know what would happen to the three orphans in Denver, and there was no use scaring the boy.

Jason asked, 'They'll what?'

'Nothin'. I'd just stay as far as you can away from do-goodin' women if I was you.'

'Plan to.' Jason grinned.

His hair was tawny and uncut, curling over his neck and ears. His eyes were light blue and his skin deeply tanned. The skin on his nose was peeling, and it was red from the sun. Tippett discovered that he liked the boy. He liked Jason's toughness and his calm confidence in himself.

Jason got up suddenly. He went to Matt beside the fire, knelt, and talked with him for several minutes. The boy, who had been on the verge of crying, seemed cheered by whatever it was Jason said to him. Jason disappeared into the darkness, and after a while he returned, carrying an armload of dry buffalo chips.

The three troopers had built their own fire a little way from the first one. They were cooking their rations apart from the civilians.

Tippett fixed a plate of bacon and fried potatoes for Jason and a smaller one for Matt, then filled a plate for himself. After eating, Jason cleaned both his own plate and Matt's with sand. He hollowed out a little place near the fire for Matt and himself, and the two lay down to sleep.

Tippett sat beside the fire for a while, smoking his pipe. He'd been about to tell Jason awhile ago that if he wasn't careful the busybodies in Denver would split the three children up or send them to an orphanage, if there was one in Denver. But even if he had warned Jason specifically, he doubted if it would have done any good. Homeless children were a kind of challenge to womenfolk. They never thought it right, or even possible, that children could take care of themselves.

And maybe they were right, he thought ruefully, as long as there were vultures like Gruber around to prey on them.

He got to his feet, went to the troopers' fire, and said, 'One of you had better stand guard. Just to make sure the Indians don't try gettin' even with us.'

One of the troopers moved out away from the fire, his rifle in his hands. Tippett turned to the other fire. He got his blanket and spread it over Jason and Matt, who already were asleep. He lay down nearby and closed his eyes.

He had a moment's worry about the strongbox filled with specie. He told himself he was being foolish, but he knew that he was not. Gruber was an outlaw. He had Charity Huntzinger as his hostage. And there were only two men on guard back at the stage depot.

Tippett got up at dawn, only to discover that Jason was up ahead of him. Jason had a fresh fire built and was hunkered beside it, warming his hands. Matt hunkered beside Jason, imitating him.

There were some cold biscuits in the gunnysack, and everyone helped themselves to these so that they would not have to take time to cook. They brought in the horses and saddled them.

Thinking about his worry last night, Tippett spoke to the troopers. 'You go back to the stage station and wait. Gruber might have some ideas about getting his hands on that strongbox. The rest of us will follow his trail.'

The troopers rode out immediately, following Coyote Creek toward the west. Tippett boosted Matt up with one of the hostlers and lifted Jason up to his own saddle, seating the boy behind him on the horse's rump. 'How's your head this morning?' he asked.

'Better.' The boy was plainly impatient to go. Tippett led out, followed by Santistevan, looking glum, as if he had not slept very well. The others came along behind. Tippett cast around for fifteen minutes before he picked up Gruber's trail.

Following, he was half-afraid every time they crested a little rise. Gruber had left the three children to die when he stole their horse and gun. He had tried to kill Jason last night.

He wouldn't be above killing Charity if he felt she was slowing him down or in his way, or even simply because she was of no further use to him.

The trail led north. Gruber had been traveling at a gallop, trying to get away from the pursuit. He had held his horse to this gait for more than a mile before he slowed him to a walk.

The sun poked up above the horizon. It felt good to Tippett, chilled from lying on the ground all night without a blanket. Suddenly Gruber's trail turned at right angles toward the west.

Tippett's uneasiness of last night returned, and his suspicions were confirmed when a couple of miles farther on, the trail turned at right angles again and headed south. Gruber was headed back toward the stage depot.

Knowing it was useless, Tippett kicked his horse into a lope. Behind him, Jason held on by putting his arms around Tippett's waist, but the boy didn't say anything.

At least, Tippett thought, there was more hope now that the little girl would be recovered alive. Gruber wanted only the strongbox. He might have used the girl last night to get his hands on it, but it wasn't likely he'd have taken her with him when he left.

CHAPTER THIRTEEN

Gruber held his hand over the terrified girl's mouth until he judged they were well out of earshot of the others. He took it away then, but when Charity began to yell, he slapped her and she stopped.

Gruber's wounded leg was a fiery area of pain. The only thing that made it bearable was the remembrance of the way he'd been able to clip Jason with his gun. He hoped he'd hit hard enough, but he doubted if he had.

He rode straight north in case they tried trailing him in spite of the darkness. Then he turned straight west. He rode for a couple of miles before he turned back south toward the stage depot.

Excitement helped dull the pain in his wounded leg. He had almost pulled it off. That strongbox filled with paper money was almost within his grasp.

He had no fear that he would be overtaken by anyone following him. What he did fear was the swift return to the stage depot of the eight men he had left behind.

Taking the little girl would therefore serve him doubly. First, she had kept them from running him down and killing him immediately. Second, he figured that taking her would probably keep the men where they were so that they could take his trail immediately when it got light enough. They would know that returning to the stage depot tonight would only cost them time when morning came.

He remembered the driver, Tippett. Tippett had been the one who had doubted his story of the Indians' kidnapping the children. And Tippett would be the first to suspect him of having designs on the money shipment.

Thinking of Tippett, he kicked his horse again into a steady lope. He kept one arm around Charity so that she wouldn't try jumping from the horse. He didn't need her now, but the time might come when he would.

He covered the ten miles to the stage depot rapidly. He was intensely relieved when he brought it into sight and saw no horses tied in front of it. Charity let out a yell, so he covered her mouth with a hand. He dismounted, dragging her off the horse with him. He didn't want to take the time to find something to gag and tie her with, so he chose a simpler expedient. He hit her on the jaw with his fist. She crumpled to the ground without a sound.

Leaving the horse, he walked toward the stage depot, rifle in hand. He walked quickly but silently. There were lights inside.

A man came out, stood on the stoop a moment to stretch, then headed for the outhouse behind the building. Gruber moved forward swiftly now, resembling nothing so

115

much as a night-hunting cat. He rounded the stage depot as the outhouse door slammed, and in seconds had taken up a position directly beside it so that he could strike the man when he emerged.

He hadn't long to wait. The man stepped outside and paused to button his pants. Gruber struck silently and without warning. He brought the gun barrel down like a club, and it struck the man squarely on the top of the head with a sodden crack.

The man collapsed the way Charity had, without a sound. The difference was that the man was dead almost instantly. Stopping to get hold of him and drag him away, Gruber recognized Ratcliff, the shotgun guard.

He laid his rifle on the ground and dragged Ratcliff far enough away so that he would not be seen by anyone else coming to the outhouse. Then he returned and picked his rifle up.

A sense of urgency prodded him. Tippett and the others might be arriving at any time, depending on whether or not Tippett had guessed what he meant to do. He hurried back to the front of the stage depot. Cautiously he approached and stared through the window. The two women were sitting at the table. The trooper who had been left here with Ratcliff was pacing back and forth. Frequently he glanced at the door, as if anxiously waiting for Ratcliff to return.

Gruber backed away. The trooper was

wearing a sidearm, and if anything made him suspicious, he could be dangerous. Gruber took a position at the corner of the building and waited. Sooner or later the trooper would come out to see where Ratcliff was.

The door of the stage depot opened finally, and at almost exactly that same instant, Charity Huntzinger regained consciousness and screeched.

The trooper stepped outside. Gruber raised his gun.

Again Charity screeched. The trooper, hatless and in shirt sleeves, plunged for the corner of the building.

Gruber fired, but too late, because the trooper had already begun to move. The bullet missed, and before Gruber could fire again, the trooper had ducked behind the building corner and disappeared.

Gruber, a sinking sensation of failure in his stomach, whirled and sprinted for the back of the building. He heard the trooper's muffled yell, 'Ratcliff! You there?'

He rounded the corner, but he turned too fast for his wounded leg. It gave way with him and dumped him to the ground.

It was fortunate for him that it did, because the trooper had apparently been waiting for him to appear. The trooper's revolver flared.

From the ground, Gruber fired too, his shot echoing that of the trooper. Both bullets missed. Gruber couldn't see the trooper clearly, but he knew the man had the same handicap. He had pinpointed his own location for the trooper by firing, and he flung himself violently to the side just as the trooper's gun flared a second time.

This bullet tore a furrow in the earth not a foot away from Gruber's head and showered him with stinging particles of dirt. Before he could bring his gun to bear again, the trooper had withdrawn.

Knowing the trooper was still standing there, Gruber began to crawl away. Out in front he could hear the women calling to Charity and could hear Charity answering. He could see his vision of all that money fading. If he didn't kill this damned trooper soon, he'd never get his hands on it.

Only darkness sheltered him. Otherwise he was exposed. But the darkness must have provided good enough concealment, because the trooper still had not fired again.

Gruber struggled painfully to his feet, keeping a watchful eye on the building corner behind which the trooper had disappeared. He limped to the other corner and headed for the front of the building.

Dimly he saw Charity approaching at a run. She hadn't seen him, hidden as he was by the shadows. She was running toward the two women standing in the doorway calling her.

He let her reach them, and watched as the older one caught the little girl in her arms and carried her inside.

He returned to the rear of the building, reasoning that if he made no sound the trooper might figure he had succeeded in killing him. He might step out from the building corner to investigate.

The only light came from the stars. It wasn't much, but by kneeling down, Gruber knew he'd be able to silhouette at least the trooper's head and shoulders against the starry sky.

Gun ready, he crouched and waited patiently. He waited almost five minutes before he heard the soft scuffing of a boot.

He raised his gun and steadied it against the building wall. He aimed at the place he figured the trooper would first appear.

Something black blotted out a few of the stars. It stopped a foot away from the sheltering corner of the building and remained still.

Gruber fired. The report was sharp and harsh. The flare illuminated the rear of the waystation briefly, the way a flash of lightning might. In that flash of light Gruber got a glimpse of the trooper. He saw the trooper's body jerk and knew he had scored a hit.

He moved forward swiftly in spite of his limp. He reached the trooper, shoved his gun muzzle against the body, and pulled the trigger a second time.

Knowing the trooper was now either dead or dying, he hurried to the front of the building again. He went to the door and stepped inside.

The older woman was holding Charity, who was crying. All three turned their heads to stare at him. Gruber asked, 'Where'd they put the box?'

Neither woman answered him. He limped across the room and struck the young one in the face. He didn't have time to argue or cajole. He didn't even have time for threats.

They must have understood just how dangerous he was. The older woman said, 'It's in that storeroom over there.'

Gruber crossed the room, watching the women out of the corner of his eye. He yanked open the door and pulled the metal strongbox out. He put down his rifle and drew his revolver. Taking careful aim, he fired at the lock, and when it failed to open, fired a second time. This time the lock came open, and Gruber flung back the lid.

The shipment was in white canvas bags, four of them. He went back into the storeroom and got a couple of gunnysacks. He put two of the money bags into one, the remaining two into the other one. He found a short piece of rope and tied the two gunnysacks together.

He picked up his rifle and carried the two gunnysacks to the door. Turning, he faced the two terrified women again.

He felt no moral barrier to killing them, and certainly two more killings weren't going to stiffen the penalty he'd pay if he was caught, because he had already killed two men.

He raised his gun. Faces ghastly, the two women and the little girl stared at him. He said, 'Bring that girl over here.'

Like a bird hypnotized by a snake, Mrs Plowman slowly complied. She put Charity down on the floor, still holding onto her hand. Gruber took it in his own. He said, 'All right, go on back where you were.'

Mrs Plowman backed away. She swallowed and croaked, 'Killing us isn't going to help. We can't follow you.'

'You can tell who took the money. And you can testify against me if I'm caught.'

'But we won't. I swear we won't.'

Gruber laughed harshly. He thumbed back the hammer of his gun. Charity suddenly pulled violently, and to keep her from getting away, he tightened his grip on her.

The young woman screamed and fainted. His aim spoiled, Gruber lowered the gun.

Angrily he hit the little girl. Stunned, she collapsed to the floor at his feet.

During that short interval, he decided against killing the two women before he left, because it would do no good. They couldn't tell the men anything they wouldn't know as soon as they found the contents of the strongbox gone. And killing two women might do him a lot of harm. Posses were just a little more anxious to capture woman-killers than they were to recover stolen money. Still holding his

121

gun, Gruber dragged Charity, half-conscious, out through the door.

He dragged her away toward the place he had left his horse. She recovered enough to walk, but she kept pulling against him, trying to get away. She screamed at the two women to help.

The older woman, Mrs Plowman, came to the door and stared after them, unable to see them but seeming to know which way they had gone. The young woman must still be unconscious, Gruber thought.

He felt like shouting with exuberance. Slung over his shoulder he had a fortune in paper money, enough to keep him in luxury for the rest of his life. He had the fastest and strongest of all the horses that had been available at this lonely waystation. In another couple of minutes he'd be mounted and on his way.

And if, by some remote chance, they did pursue, and if, by some remoter chance, they overtook him finally, he had a hostage to keep them from taking him.

The little girl continued to scream for help. Gruber said harshly, 'Shut up, damn you, 'less'n you want me to hit you again!'

Fear quieted the little girl. Gruber reached his horse. He lifted her up and painfully mounted behind her. He was bathed with sweat when he hit the saddle, but he was laughing in spite of his weakness and his pain. He was rich! Goddamnit, finally he was rich!

122

CHAPTER FOURTEEN

Mott, the corporal, led the other two troopers straight toward the stage depot, following the general course of Coyote Creek. They were limited to the speed of the horse inherited from Gruber, and so did not reach the place until morning.

The building was between them and the body of their comrade, so it was not seen until they had drawn their horses to a halt in front, not until the red-eyed women came out, that they knew anything was wrong.

Miss Jane Newton seemed to be wholly demoralized. Mrs Plowman, though red-eyed, was composed. She said, 'He was here. He killed Mr Ratcliff and your friend, stole the money, and left.'

Mott dismounted and tied his horse. The others followed suit. Mott asked, 'Where's Simpson's body, ma'am?'

'Out in back. We tried to bring him in, but he was too heavy for us.'

'Yes, ma'am.' Mott walked around the building, and the others followed him.

Mott knew how bad was the trouble he was in. He had been assigned to escort the stagecoach and to guard the money it was carrying. Now the money was gone, Simpson was dead, and he was going to be called to account for both.

He knelt beside Simpson and touched his face. The trooper's flesh was cold. Mott felt a touch of flaring anger at Gruber as he stared down at Simpson's face.

Simpson had been a good trooper, with more than ten years of loyal service. He'd have been a sergeant long ago if he hadn't liked the liquor and the women quite so well. He was a big and handsome man who had always had a ready laugh and who had been dependable in a pinch. Mott felt responsible for his death. He could—and should—have refused to go along on the rescue mission last night. He should have stayed here to guard the money. If he had, it might still be safe and Simpson might be alive.

He'd be called to account for both the loss of the money and Simpson's death when they reached Denver City. In the meantime, Simpson had to be buried, and so did the shotgun guard. If he and the two privates with him took care of that immediately, they'd be ready to go after Gruber as soon as Tippett and the others arrived.

There was a small lean-to at one side of the waystation. Mott discovered two shovels inside. He carried them up the slope behind the stage station, and the other two troopers followed, one carrying Simpson's shoulders, the other his feet. They laid him down and went back for Ratcliff.

Mott emptied Simpson's pockets. When the two men laid Ratcliff's body down, he went through the guard's pockets similarly. He marked out two graves, and the troopers set to work. Mott carried the two dead men's meager belongings back down to the waystation, took them inside, and put them on the table. 'Did he still have the little girl with him?' he asked.

Mrs Plowman nodded.

The strongbox still lay where Gruber had left it. Mott stared at it for an instant, his stomach feeling empty. This was sure as hell going to cost him his stripes, and maybe a stretch in the guardhouse, too. He asked, 'Are there a couple of blankets around here that I can wrap them in?'

Mrs Plowman got him two. The other woman, young but prim-looking, just sat staring blankly at the window. Mott said, 'When we get through, would you say some words over them?'

'Of course.'

Mott nodded. Taking the blankets, he went outside and back up the hill. Thereafter, he relieved the other troopers, each in turn, at intervals, until the graves were done. With their help, he wrapped Simpson and Ratcliff in the blankets. He arranged ropes under them so that they could be lowered into the graves. Then he walked down to the stage station and asked Mrs Plowman if she would come. The young woman, Jane Newton, hung back until

Mrs Plowman, a little sharply, told her to come along.

At the graveside, Mrs Plowman opened the Bible to a place already selected and read from it. Mott and the other two stood, hats in hand, and listened until she had finished.

The three troopers were filling in the graves when Tippett and the others rode into sight. They bypassed the waystation and rode straight to the graves.

Tippett's face was grim. 'Ratcliff and Simpson?' he asked.

'Yes, sir. Ratcliff was hit on the head. Simpson was shot.'

'And the strongbox has been broken open and the money's gone?'

'Yes, sir.'

'Did he leave the little girl?'

'No, sir. He took her with him.'

Tippett had the older boy in the saddle in front of him. One of the other men had the smaller boy propped up in front of him. Tippett said, 'Finish up as quick as you can. We'll get some provisions and be ready to go in fifteen or twenty minutes.'

'What about the women?'

Tippett glanced at the station agent. 'Maybe you'd better stay with them.'

Milton nodded.

The new arrivals turned and rode down to the waystation. They dismounted and went inside. Almost frantically Mott began

126

shoveling earth into one of the graves. Panting and short of breath, he said, 'Hurry up. The only chance we got of stayin' out of the guard-house is getting that goddamn money back.'

* * *

They rode out an hour before noon, Tippett leading, Jason following and riding his own horse. Behind Jason rode Mott, and behind him the other two troopers. Then came Santistevan, and bringing up the rear, the two stage-station hostlers.

Jason Huntzinger looked back steadily until he could no longer see the tiny, scared figure of four-year-old Matt. Then he turned his face in the direction they were riding, his thin back ramrod-straight.

* * *

Matt, his face streaked with tears, tried to run after his brother once, but Jane Newton ran after him, caught him, and brought him back. She led him firmly inside and tried to console him, without success. Milton, watching, said, 'We'd all better keep an eye on that boy, or he's goin' to try runnin' after them.'

Milton had never had children of his own, but he liked kids. He wondered what was going to happen to these three, assuming that Tippett and the others were able to get the girl

127

back unhurt.

They couldn't take care of themselves. The older boy, Jason, while able and self-sufficient, couldn't support himself, let alone the other two. They'd have to be sent to an orphanage, if there was one in Denver, or split up and taken by families who wanted them.

In midafternoon, Milton heard a shout. Going to the door, he saw a line of wagons approaching from the east. All were heavily loaded, their loads covered with canvas, lashed down tightly.

There were seven wagons in all. They pulled to a dusty halt in front of the stage waystation. The drivers set their brakes and climbed to the ground. They trooped inside, and Milton got several bottles of whiskey out, and glasses.

Milton didn't tell them anything about the robbery, but they couldn't miss the coach sitting out in front. Finally one of them asked, 'What's that coach doing here?'

Milton said, 'Long story.'

'We got time.'

Milton told them what had happened. Before he had finished, Mrs Plowman came forward and spoke to the teamster. 'Could we ride with you? We were on that coach, but no telling when it will be going on. And there isn't another due for several days.'

The man hesitated. He noticed Jane Newton standing back, and apparently without noticing the firm set of her mouth and the

128

disapproving look in her eyes over the whiskey bottles, nodded. 'Her too?'

Mrs Plowman turned her head, 'Jane, do you want to go on to Denver with these men?'

'If they're not going to sit here drinking all afternoon.'

The teamster looked suddenly as if he regretted agreeing to take the two, but he was committed and could not back out. He got to his feet. 'All right. Come on.' He looked at Mrs Plowman. 'You can ride with me, ma'am.'

Her eyes twinkled as she nodded. The man asked, 'What about the boy? Is he hers?' in a skeptical tone.

Mrs Plowman shook her head. 'He's an orphan.'

'You bringing him too?'

'Yes.'

Matt suddenly pulled his hand away from Jane. He bolted for the door and was through it and gone before anyone could move. The teamster, slow to react, was ten feet behind Jane Newton going through the door.

Matt was racing away in the direction Jason and the men had gone. Jane Newton, holding up her skirts, raced after him. The teamster asked, 'What's he runnin' for?'

'He's frightened. An outlaw kidnapped his sister as a hostage, and his older brother is with the men pursuing him. He wants to stay until they get back.'

'What's wrong with that? Why can't he stay?'

129

'Because the child needs caring for, that's why. His older brother is only twelve and his sister is only eight. Those three children can't possibly take care of themselves.'

'So who's going to take care of them?'

'Somebody will, I have no doubt, though it's not likely anyone will take all three.'

'Don't the kids have anything to say about it?'

Mrs Plowman faced him exasperatedly. 'They're not old enough to know what's good for them.'

'Maybe they know enough to want to stay together.' He was staring out across the prairie. The little boy had run several hundred yards before he ran out of breath. Jane Newton finally caught him, seized his hand, and dragged him back toward the stage depot. The little boy pulled away, and finally she stopped, turned him over her knee, and paddled him. She put him down, and he promptly kicked her in the shin and broke away again.

Mrs Plowman glanced at the teamster. He was big and bearded, but his beard didn't hide his grin. 'Spunky little devil, ain't he?'

'He needs discipline, that's what he needs. It looks to me like he's grown up half-wild.'

The teamster didn't reply. Jane Newton caught Matt again and paddled him a second time. She returned toward the waystation, dragging him along by force. The teamster's

130

voice was cold. 'I said you could go with us, and I reckon I'll stick by that. But we're leavin' in five minutes, and if you ain't ready then, we're goin' on.'

He walked to his wagon and began circling it, checking brakes and wheels. Finished with that, he checked his teams and their harness to make sure nothing was chafing them.

Jane Newton reached the stage station disheveled and out of breath. She was glad to turn Matt, still out of breath, over to Mrs Plowman, who gripped his hand and held on tight. Once they got well down the road toward Denver, Mrs Plowman thought, he'd settle down and stop trying to get away.

She told herself that she'd find him a decent home. Someplace where he'd be kept clean and well-fed, with people who would send him to school as soon as he was old enough. If he stayed with his brother, he'd grow up like an animal, and when he was grown, would probably be an outlaw like that filthy Gruber character.

She allowed the teamster to help her up onto the seat of his wagon, which was at the column's head. She settled Matt onto her lap, holding him firmly with an arm encircling him.

Matt, for all his terror, didn't cry. He held himself tense, ready to leap down and run if the opportunity ever came.

CHAPTER FIFTEEN

For a long time after they had ridden away from the waystation and after it had disappeared from sight behind them, Jason could still see Matt's tearful face and hear his cries in his mind. He felt as if he had abandoned Matt, and he was sure Matt felt that way too.

Matt wasn't old enough to understand much more than that everyone had gone away and left him alone. His father. His mother. Charity. And finally Jason, on whom he had depended most.

Jason felt like crying himself. He caught himself wishing that the men from the waystation had just left them with the Indians. At least there'd have been no question of splitting them up. They'd have been together, well fed and clothed, pretty much let alone and allowed to do what they wanted to. Eventually they'd have learned the Indians' language and would have been able to converse with them.

But there was no use thinking about what might have been. He stared at the coach driver's back ahead of him. Tippett had located Gruber's trail almost immediately after leaving the stage station, and now he was following it like a hound.

Jason liked Tippett. The big man was kind, and it was obvious that he liked kids. Jason thought Tippett particularly liked him, but that might have been because he particularly wanted Tippett to like him. Tippett was the kind of man he wanted to be like himself someday.

He rode closer and asked, 'You reckon Matt will be all right?'

'Sure he will. Them two women will take good care of him.'

'How long will it take us to catch up with Gruber?'

Tippett turned his head. 'Trail's more'n twelve hours old. He's got the best horse. I won't fool you, boy. It could take awhile.'

'You think he'll hurt Charity?' What he really meant was would Gruber kill Charity, but he hadn't been able to bring himself to put it into so many words.

'Naw. Why should he? He'll keep her until he figures he don't need her no more, and then he'll let her go.'

For the first time Jason paid notice to the direction they were traveling. Straight west, it was, toward Denver and the Continental Divide beyond. He strained his eyes, trying to see the lift of mountains ahead, but they still were too far away.

What would he do, he asked himself, if they found Charity lying dead beside the trail? The very thought made his throat grow tight and made a blur come into his eyes. He wasn't going to think of that anymore, he firmly told

133

himself. Charity was going to be all right. So was Matt. They'd been worried several days ago about Matt's wound, but that had turned out all right, hadn't it? And this was going to turn out all right, too.

Tippett held his horse to a steady trot. After a while he said, 'He slowed down some. For a while after leavin' the waystation he kept his horse at a lope. I figure the critter got all sweated up. He pulled him back to a walk.'

Jason found that encouraging. Tippett was holding a steady trot and had ever since they'd left the waystation. Jason knew their horses could maintain the trot all day long without tiring. If Gruber kept his mount at a walk, they'd slowly begin overtaking him.

Behind Jason, the others had strung out until the column was nearly a quarter-mile long. Mott, the corporal, was fifty yards behind Jason, but Jason had kept the interval between himself and Tippett to less than a dozen feet so that they could talk.

Jason didn't need to be told that they were doing everything they could. They were pushing the horses as much as they dared. They were following Gruber's trail, and it wasn't likely anything was going to happen to blot it out. There were a few clouds hanging in the west, but they were not threatening. He called, 'Where you reckon he's headed?'

'Mountains. Gold camps, probably. Or maybe he's just figurin' on crossin' them and goin' on to California.'

'What if he reaches the mountains before we catch up with him?'

'What if he does?'

'Ain't we likely to lose his trail?'

Tippett turned his head. 'He ain't going to reach them mountains before we catch up with him. You just get that thought out of your head.'

But Jason was worried, and he was scared. He asked, 'What if them women take Matt on to Denver with them whilst we're gone?'

'They can't do that. There isn't another stage until next week.'

That was reassuring to Jason. He didn't need to worry about Matt, anyway. Only Charity.

Tippett returned his attention to the trail. Jason occupied himself by studying the ground similarly. Someday he wanted to be able to trail the way Tippett did, and now was a good time to begin learning.

The afternoon dragged slowly by. The sun settled toward the horizon in the west. It shone almost directly into their eyes now, hot and bright. It seemed impossible that it had snowed so furiously less than a week ago. Now grass was beginning to poke up, fresh and green, from the sun-drenched ground.

Tippett picked up the pace to a lope. After half a mile he slowed again to a trot. After another half-mile he picked up the pace again to a lope.

Jason felt better every time they loped. But as the afternoon wore to a close, he began wondering why Tippett was hurrying.

The sun dropped even lower in the sky. And suddenly Jason understood why Tippett was hurrying. The sun's rim had dropped behind something there in the west, something well above the level of the plain. Straining his eyes, Jason studied that horizon.

Ghostly and nearly invisible because of haze, distance, and dust, the mighty Rockies lifted their hoary heads. The sun was now halfway hidden behind one of the tallest of the peaks, and its dying golden rays put a sudden and unexpected shine on a snowfield near the mountain's top.

Jason felt an involuntary shiver run along his spine. He had wanted to see the Rocky Mountains all his life, and now, like a specter rising out of the plain, he saw them finally. Their nearness explained Tippett's hurrying. Tippett had seen them long before Jason had, and Tippett was as afraid as Jason was that Gruber would reach them and manage to hide his trail from the men pursuing him.

The sun disappeared behind the peak, and its dying glow silhouetted the great long line of mountains that marched from north to south for as far as the eye could see. Briefly the clouds flamed gold, and then gray crept across the sky.

Tippett trailed for as long as he could. Finally he pulled his horse to a halt and stepped to the ground. The others caught up and dismounted. Each man began caring for his mount. It would be a dry camp, because no watercourse was in sight, but each man had a canteen, and the horses had been watered in late afternoon and would need no more tonight.

Jason slid to the ground, trying not to show the deep disappointment he felt. If they camped here tonight, they would never overtake Gruber and Charity. The man would reach the mountains and would be able to hide his trail on the rocky ground.

With their horses cared for and picketed, the men scattered to gather buffalo chips for a fire. Jason brought in a load and hesitated beside Tippett, who was kindling the fire. He said glumly, 'He's goin' to get away from us, ain't he?'

Tippett didn't answer immediately. When he finally did reply, he didn't try to sugar-coat the truth. He said, 'Looks like it.'

'Ain't there nothing we can do?'

'I don't know what it'd be.'

Jason said, 'He's been goin' straight all day. Don't you reckon we could take a chance that he'll keep goin' straight?'

Tippett considered that. Finally he said, 'If we bet on that and turn out wrong, we'll never see the man again. And if he left your sister on the trail, nobody would ever find her.'

Jason thought about that carefully. Finally

137

an idea occurred to him. 'What if you and me was to go on tonight? What if the others was to stay with the trail?'

Tippett kept adding dry buffalo chips to the fire until it was burning well. Finally he said, 'We'll do it on one condition—that there's somebody among the rest of 'em that can trail.'

Jason stared around impatiently, waiting for the other men to come in. Finally they had all brought in the loads they had gathered, and Tippett asked, 'Any of you able to read trail?'

Nobody answered immediately, and Jason's heart sank. Finally one of the waystation hostlers said, 'If you mean this trail, I reckon I can follow it. At least, until he gets to the mountains.'

Tippett asked, 'You willing to try?'

The man nodded. 'Why?'

'This boy and me figure on goin' on tonight. We can't follow trail, but if he keeps going straight west the way he's been doin', maybe we can pick him up again when it gets light.'

The hostler said, 'Good idea. We'll watch for you.'

Jason headed for his horse, but Tippett stopped him. 'Whoa, now. If these horses are goin' to be traveling all night, they need some rest. So do we. You lay down and shut your eyes, and I'll call you when grub's ready.'

Jason did not protest. He lay down and closed his eyes. He remembered Matt's tear-streaked face and hoped his brother was all

138

right. There was no reason he shouldn't be, he told himself. There were two women with him to care for him. Charity's situation was more precarious. He knew how vicious Gruber was and knew the outlaw wouldn't hesitate about killing Charity or abandoning her. The only encouraging thing was that he had not done it so far.

He finally dropped off to sleep, and it seemed only a few minutes before Tippett was shaking him awake. He got up, went to the fire, and accepted the plate Tippett handed him. He wolfed down the food.

While he ate, Tippett brought the horses in and saddled them. Then he took part of the food in one of the gunnysacks and tied it to his saddle horn. He boosted Jason up, mounted himself, and led off toward the west.

Except for the starlight, it was black as pitch. Tippett was apparently guiding himself by the stars, because Jason could see him glancing up occasionally. Tippett kept his horse at a steady trot. Once he was forced to detour a tall, flat-topped butte, but when he was around it, he lined out straight west once more.

Jason wasn't normally a worrier, but tonight he discovered he was worried both about Matt and about Charity. He wondered why he was so worried about Matt. The boy was safe at the waystation, with two capable women to care for him. They might not overwhelm him with affection, but they'd take good care of him

139

physically. He got to wondering if the Indians would attack the waystation in revenge for the attack that had been made on their village by the whites.

He considered that for a while, then shook his head. It was doubtful if the Indians would be anxious to renew that conflict, having suffered so heavily in the attack on their village earlier. They'd be content to lick their wounds, bury their dead, pack up their village, and go away.

But Jason couldn't stop his thoughts, and being the oldest, and responsible now for both Matt and Charity, he couldn't help worrying about them.

CHAPTER SIXTEEN

Conscious of the need to conserve the horses' strength, Tippett held them to a steady walk. They were going to be called upon to travel almost constantly until Gruber was caught. They would need long rest periods, frequent stops, occasional rubdowns, and the opportunity to graze as they traveled.

He could hear Jason's horse coming along behind. The boy kept the horse close to Tippett's, probably for reassurance and companionship. Briefly Tippett wondered what the boy's father had been like.

140

In his mind he came up with a picture of a man nothing at all like Len Huntzinger. Jason's fierce independence did not suggest a defeated father.

A sudden, new idea struck Tippett like a thunderbolt. Why couldn't he and Mary take these kids? They'd always wanted kids, but for some reason they'd never been able to have any of their own.

God knew the kids needed someone to take care of them. Jobs weren't exactly plentiful in Denver or in the mining communities west of it. It was hard for an able grown man to make a living, doubly hard if he had a family. The best Jason could hope to do, even if he was successful in keeping his brother and sister with him, was to eke out a bare existence for the three of them.

And he wouldn't be successful in keeping them both with him. Tippett remembered Mrs Plowman and Jane Newton. Those two would never stand for it. They'd have the kids split up half a day after they reached Denver with them.

Furthermore, there was a good chance the kids would go to people interested only in the work the kids could do in return for their room and board.

Tippett wondered what Mary would have to say. He visualized her, realizing suddenly and with mild surprise that she wasn't as slim as she used to be. She had grown matronly, but her smile was still the same, and so was her generous disposition. He needn't wonder how Mary would take to the idea. She'd be as crazy about the kids as he would be himself.

He turned his head to ask Jason what he thought of the idea, then turned it back without saying anything. He owed it to Mary to give her a chance to say what she thought first. And it wasn't fair to Jason to ask him to make such a decision while he was still so desperately worried about Charity.

The hours dragged slowly past. At what he judged to be midnight, Tippett stopped. He unsaddled his horse and rubbed his back with the saddle blanket, afterward fanning him with it. As soon as Jason saw what Tippett was doing, he followed suit. Tippett took the bit out of his horse's mouth, but left the bridle on, with reins dragging. He released the horse, which immediately began to graze.

Jason also released his horse to graze. He paced nervously back and forth until Tippett said, 'Just as well lay down and take it easy. The horses have got to have an hour's rest.'

Jason paced back and forth a few more times. Then he sat down on the ground close to Tippett. He said, 'Waitin's hard.'

'Uh-huh.'

'You reckon we'll be able to pick up his trail tomorrow?'

'We'll try.'

'How?'

142

'Well, when it gets light, I'm goin' to angle off one way and you're goin' to angle off the other. Unless he just plain changed direction, I don't figure we could be more'n a couple of miles off course. Whoever finds his trail can fire his gun.'

Jason considered that.

Tippett said curiously, 'You never did tell me the whole story about how you met Gruber.'

'He must've crossed our trail in the snow. He come up on us whilst we was camped. I was goin' to run him off with Pa's gun, but he told us he didn't mean us no harm, and besides, he said, he had food enough for all of us. He cooked some up, but when he was finished, he just went and got our horse and gun and walked away with 'em.'

'What'd you do?'

'I ran after him. He knocked me down a couple of times, and after that he just stayed ahead of me until I wore out.'

'Then what?'

'I walked back to camp. I couldn't see no way we could stay alive without that horse and gun. So I set out to follow him an' get 'em back.'

'You were able to trail him?'

'There was still some of that snow layin' on the ground. It wasn't hard to follow the trail he left, even in the dark. I kep' goin' until I caught up with him.'

Tippett was grinning faintly to himself.

Jason said, 'I sneaked in and took the guns. When he woke up I made him lie down on the ground. I knew I'd never get up on the horse with them guns and get away as long as he was able to stop me, so I hit him on the head.'

'How'd he catch up with you a second time?'

'Well, I never did take his horse. Just ours. And all the guns. I figured he'd go on and just forget about us, but he didn't. He came after us again.'

'And that time you shot him?'

'Him and his horse both. I didn't feel right about it, knowin' I'd be to blame if he died, but I didn't know what else to do. He'd made it plain he didn't mean to leave us alone. I figured it was him or us.'

'You hungry?'

'Some.'

Tippett dug into the gunnysack and brought out some dry biscuits. He gave a couple to Jason, along with the canteen. 'Tell me about your pa.'

There was a moment's silence. Finally Jason said, 'I reckon Pa was the unluckiest man that ever lived. Ever'thing he done turned sour. If he got a good crop, the hail and wind would come along and knock it flat. If he put up grain for the winter, the mice got into it. A bear killed our cow once by scarin' her so bad she run right into a tree. It was like that all the time. But Pa worked. He always worked hard, an' Ma

144

did too.'

'He must've been a pretty good man to raise a kid like you.'

Jason didn't answer that, probably because it embarrassed him. He stretched out on the ground and stared up at the stars. 'How far away you reckon them stars are?'

'They say millions and millions of miles.'

Jason was silent, considering that. Tippett knew what he was thinking. It was hard for a boy to visualize a million miles when he could walk only ten or fifteen miles a day. Jason asked, 'You reckon they'll ever fall down on us?'

'Nope.'

'How far you reckon Gruber is ahead of us?'

'I'll be better able to tell tomorrow when we find his trail again.'

Jason got up and began pacing again. Finally Tippett got to his feet. 'All right. Saddle up. I guess we can go on.'

Both caught their horses, put the bits back in, and saddled them. Again Tippett led out at a walk. The horses kept grabbing mouthfuls of grass occasionally as they walked, and neither Tippett nor Jason tried to keep them from doing so.

After about an hour's silence Jason asked, 'How far you reckon them mountains was?'

'You mean when the sun went down?'

'Uh-huh.'

'Hundred miles, maybe.'

145

'And how far we come since then?'

'Walkin' the horses, I'd say less'n ten.'

'Can't we go faster?'

'Beat ourselves if we do. Gruber's horse is carryin' double weight. I figure he's enough scared of bein' caught that he's pushin' his horse just about all he can. His horse'll play out before ours does.'

'But what if he gets to the mountains first?'

'Then we lose him. But he ain't going to.'

'What if he gets another horse?'

'Don't see how he can. Ain't no ranches this far out. We ain't nowhere near the stage road.'

'But...'

'You calm down, boy. I know you're worried, but worryin' ain't going to help. Hell, boy, I'm worried too. How you think I'm going to explain losin' all that money and lettin' Ratcliff get killed, to say nothing of that trooper Gruber killed?'

'They can't blame you.'

Tippett said, 'They can and they will. I wasn't supposed to be off chasing Indians. I was supposed to be drivin' stage.'

They did not converse after that. Tippett dozed in his saddle occasionally, but never long enough to let his horse get off the straight line toward the west. It seemed forever before the first faint line of gray appeared behind them, and it seemed another eternity before the sun came up.

As soon as it did, Tippett said, 'You head off

146

that way.' He pointed. 'And I'll go this way. Watch the ground close, and don't ride no place where a trail won't show up plain. Fire your gun if you find anything.'

Jason nodded, immediately reining his horse in the direction Tippett had pointed out to him. Tippett angled off the other way, keeping a close eye on the ground.

Jason grew smaller as he got farther and farther away. Tippett was beginning to wonder if he had not miscalculated disastrously, when he finally found the trail. He immediately drew his rifle from the saddle scabbard, raised the muzzle, and fired it.

The report rolled flat across the land. Tippett narrowed his eyes, studying Jason's tiny figure. It seemed like almost a minute before Jason turned his horse, and Tippett supposed it had taken that long for the report to reach his ears.

Having satisfied himself that Jason was coming, Tippett dismounted and knelt beside the trail. He studied it with narrowed eyes.

The ground was still damp from the snowfall of almost a week ago, damp at least where clumps of grass and brush had shaded it from the sun. The prints of Gruber's horse in these damp spots were plain, and, Tippett discovered with some relief, sharp.

Tippett had known a lot of men more expert at reading trail than he was. He found himself wishing he had one of them with him now.

147

Intently he studied the tracks, allowing for the fact that during the night there would be less drying and less sloughing off than during the day in bright sunlight. He finally came to the conclusion, as Jason rode up, that this trail had been made yesterday evening just before the sun went down.

Jason dismounted and hurried to him. 'Can you tell how far ahead of us he is?'

'Not as close as I'd like. But I figure this trail was made yesterday afternoon.'

'Then if he camped, we ought to run onto his camp pretty soon.'

'Yep.' Tippett mounted his horse and headed west again, following the trail. Glancing back once, he saw that Jason was eagerly scanning the land ahead.

Once Jason said, 'I don't suppose you can tell whether or not he still had Charity.'

'No. But as soon as we find his camp, we'll know.'

'What if . . .' Jason apparently could not go on.

But Tippett knew what he meant. He said, 'If he left her along the trail someplace, the others will pick her up.' He didn't even hint at it, but he believed that if Gruber did leave the little girl behind, she would not be alive.

An hour passed. Another. Jason broke the silence, saying, 'Hadn't we'd ought to've found their camp?'

'Not yet. They could've traveled four or five

148

hours before they stopped. I could have been wrong about the time.'

Ahead now, Tippett spotted the trees and brush that marked the bed of a stream. He didn't say anything, but he kicked his horse into a trot.

They reached the watercourse, a narrow trickle in a wide dry bed of sand. On the near bank Tippett found the place where Gruber had camped last night. Before getting down, he rode on far enough to ascertain that Gruber had gone on this morning and was still several hours ahead.

He returned then and dismounted. Jason was already on the ground, kneeling and studying the tracks. He looked up, strong relief in his face. 'I found her footprints. She's still all right.'

Tippett wanted to stop here and rest the horses for a while, but he knew that stopping now would be too hard on the boy. He mounted and led out, with Jason following eagerly.

CHAPTER SEVENTEEN

All day the two continued westward, saving the horses as much as possible by holding them to a steady walk. Every two or three hours Tippett stopped, dismounted, and the two

149

unsaddled and cooled their horses' backs. At each halt Tippett knelt and carefully studied the tracks of Gruber's horse. It was apparent to Tippett that Gruber was now walking his horse too. It was also apparent that the horse was tired.

That wasn't surprising, considering the way Gruber had ridden him at first, also considering the fact that he was carrying two. At sundown the trail appeared to be no more than a couple of hours old.

Tippett stopped in a little hollow and once more unsaddled to cool his horse's back. Jason followed suit, looking anxiously at him. 'How close are we now?' he asked finally.

'Couple of hours, looks like.'

'Can't we go on?'

'Too risky. If he seen us, he'd keep goin' all night. This way, I figure he'll stop. His horse is near played out. He's been walkin' him all day, but the critter's got to have some rest or die.'

'Then what are we goin' to do?'

'I figure we'll stop here until it's dark. Then we'll go on. Chances are we'll spot his campfire and be able to take him by surprise.'

'What if he don't build no fire?'

'No reason why he shouldn't. He likely thinks he's lost us by now. Besides, he's still got your sister, Charity.'

Tippett got the gunnysack and took out some bacon and the last of the biscuits. He built a fire of buffalo chips, which was nearly

150

smokeless, and put the bacon on to fry. Jason, without being told, went after more buffalo chips. It was nearly dark when he returned.

Tippett took the bacon out and fried the biscuits in the grease. The two sat down to eat. Jason wolfed his food, anxious to be finished and on the trail again.

But Tippett took his time. If Gruber had camped, there was no hurry about catching up with him.

At last, nearly an hour after the sky had turned dark, Tippett saddled up his horse. Jason eagerly did likewise. The pair mounted and headed west again, toward the jagged peaks that, at sundown today, had looked as if they were no more than a dozen miles away.

They rode steadily for more than two hours. Frequently Jason asked, 'Hadn't we ought to've seen somethin' by now?'

Each time Tippett replied, 'Easy, son. We will.'

'What if he didn't build no fire?'

'It's chilly once it gets dark. He'd of built a fire unless he knew we was close. And I don't see how he could've known that.'

They went on. Finally Tippett stopped on top of a low ridge and began meticulously studying the land ahead. He saw it finally, more a glow than a bright spot of light, due probably to the way buffalo chips burn. As he watched, the fire turned yellow, stayed that way for several moments, then faded to a bluish glow again. Gruber must have added fuel to it or stirred it, Tippett thought.

He pointed it out to Jason. 'There they are.'

Jason didn't say anything, but Tippett was close enough to him to sense the boy's trembling. He himself felt a vast relief. There, ahead, were not only Gruber and the little girl. There, also, was the stolen money, whose recovery meant so much to Tippett's future and to the troopers who also had been charged with guarding it. Tippett said, 'All right, let's go.'

He noticed, before mounting, which way the wind was blowing, and changed direction so that he could come up on Gruber's camp with the wind blowing across between him and the camp. He didn't want to risk Gruber's horse scenting his and Jason's horses, and he didn't want to risk their horses scenting Gruber's animal. Jason was now utterly silent, but Tippett could hear the sound of his breathing occasionally when he got close.

They finally reached a spot within a hundred yards of the camp. Here Tippett stopped. He dismounted and hunkered down, and the boy squatted silently at his side.

Gruber was still limping around in camp. The little girl was on the ground beside the fire, either sleeping or pretending to.

As they watched, Gruber got his blanket. He built up the fire once more and then stretched himself out, putting Charity between the fire and himself. He had a short piece of rope, and he tied one end to one of Charity's ankles, the other end to one of his own. Tippett breathed, 'He ain't taking no chances, is he?'

'She'd get away if she could. She'd take his horse.'

Tippett was silent, wondering what to do. Jason asked, 'How we going to get her away from him? If we go in and try takin' him, he'll grab her an' use her for a shield.'

That was exactly the conclusion to which Tippett had come. He didn't see how they could take Tippett as long as he was roped to the little girl.

Jason said, 'Let me sneak in an' cut her loose. Once we're away from him, you can capture him.'

Tippett considered that. It was the only solution that made any sense. But they'd have to wait long enough to be sure Gruber was asleep.

Tippett noticed that Gruber was using his saddlebags for a pillow, and that both rifle and revolver were close to him. He said, 'All right. But we've got to give him time to get to sleep.'

After that, both were silent for a long, long time. Gruber turned over once. After what Tippett judged to be thirty minutes, he got stiffly to his feet, and touching Jason on the shoulder, moved carefully and silently closer to the camp.

Gruber hadn't moved for nearly twenty

minutes. Tippett stopped a hundred feet away, scarcely daring now to breathe.

Faintly the sound of Gruber's snores came to him. He shifted his attention to the little girl, wondering if she too were asleep. He doubted it, and it would help if she was not. She wouldn't be startled when Jason crept close, and she would make no sudden sounds.

Finally Tippett whispered to the boy, 'All right, go on, but be careful, and if he moves, you freeze.'

'What if he wakes up?'

'You run. I'll take over then.'

'I can't—'

'You run. He'll kill you if he gets a chance.'

Jason didn't answer him. He started to move away, but Tippett caught him by the arm. He said, 'Boy, I want your word.'

Jason hesitated. Finally he said reluctantly, 'Yes, sir.'

'You'll do what I said?'

'Yes, sir. If he wakes up.'

'You got a knife?'

'Yes, sir, but it ain't very sharp.'

'Then take mine.' Tippett handed the boy his pocketknife.

Jason moved away, putting each foot down carefully and testing it before putting his full weight on it. The distance wasn't far. Jason circled slightly so that he could creep up on the sleeping pair with the fire between them and him.

Tippett walked to his horse and slipped his rifle out of the saddle boot. He knew if he had to fire, he'd need as much accuracy as possible. The light was bad; Gruber would be moving fast, and the little girl might be close to him.

He sat down on the ground, braced his elbows against his knees, and brought the rifle to his shoulder. He sighted it on Gruber, satisfied that in this position he could keep it steady. Carefully, then, muffling the sound with one of his hands, he jacked a cartridge in.

Jason had halved the distance to the fire. Tippett realized he was holding his breath. Slowly, step by careful step, the boy moved closer.

Suddenly Gruber stopped snoring. Jason froze. Restlessly Gruber turned over, and now he was facing the fire instead of away from it.

For what seemed an eternity, Jason stood frozen. Finally Gruber sighed and began to snore again.

Slowly, slowly, Jason crept closer, circling so he could reach Charity's feet and cut the rope. Charity raised her head.

Tippett held his breath. If she cried out...

But she did not. Apparently she had recognized Jason immediately. Jason moved quickly now, though still making no noise. He reached Charity's feet, knelt, and being careful not to pull against Gruber's leg, cut the rope.

He remained there, crouched, knife in hand, while Charity carefully eased herself away.

Only when she was a full twenty feet away did Jason move. Tippett realized with some admiration that the boy had remained, ready to attack Gruber with the pocketknife if he awakened and threatened Charity.

Tippett stayed where he was until both Jason and Charity had reached him. Charity was trembling violently, and he was afraid she was going to get hysterical. He moved in swiftly, rifle ready and cocked.

Gruber awakened when Tippett was still ten feet away. He grabbed instinctively for his gun.

Tippett covered the last ten feet in a couple of swift strides. He kicked as Gruber's gun came up, knocking the weapon out of Gruber's hand. Gruber grabbed for the rifle.

Tippett, suddenly thinking of Ratcliff, swung the barrel of the rifle savagely.

It connected with Gruber just above the ear. He fell like a sledged steer, his head at the edge of the fire, and lay still. Tippett smelled singeing hair and stooped to pull him away.

Gruber was unconscious. Tippett turned his head and called, 'You can come in now, kids.'

Out in the darkness he could hear Charity suddenly give way. Hysterical cries seemed torn from her, and accompanying them he could hear Jason's words as the boy tried unsuccessfully to comfort her.

He walked to the horses and led them back to the fire. He got the rope from his saddle, and despite the rope's stiffness, tied Gruber's hands and feet.

Jason and Charity had come to the fire. Charity was still sniffling, but her hysterics had stopped. Jason asked, 'How long you reckon it'll take us to get back to the stage station? Matt's probably thinkin' we ran out on him.'

'Couple of days. But I doubt if Matt'll be there when we get back. Another stage was due to go through yesterday. I figure them two women will have taken Matt on to Denver with them. No need to worry about it, though. We'll find him all right when we get there.' He was looking into Gruber's saddlebags, checking to see that all the money was there, and so did not see Jason's face.

Gruber groaned as consciousness returned. He saw Tippett, and saw Jason, and he began to curse the boy vitriolically. Tippett said harshly, 'Shut your mouth or I'll stuff something into it!'

Gruber grumbled, but he stopped cursing. Tippett said, 'Better get some sleep, you two. We'll be starting back at dawn tomorrow.'

Neither Jason nor Charity said anything. Tippett watched them settle down near the fire. He threw Gruber's blanket over the man. He staked out the horses and then lay down to sleep himself.

He was tired, and he went almost immediately to sleep. Gruber struggled with the ropes awhile, until both ankles and wrists were raw. Then he closed his eyes and went back to sleep.

Jason waited until both Tippett and Gruber were snoring lustily. Then he touched Charity, and both children got up silently. Jason rolled their blankets.

He took a small amount of food out of the gunnysack Tippett had been carrying. He bridled and saddled the horse he had ridden here. He boosted Charity up onto the horse's back.

He led the animal a couple of hundred yards away from camp before he climbed up himself. Then, walking the horse, he headed toward the faint, jagged line of mountains in the west.

He knew what those two women would do with Matt. They'd either put him in an orphanage or give him to some family, maybe even a family that was just passing through. If he and Charity didn't get to Denver fast, they might never see Matt again.

Well aware of how worn out the horse he was riding was, Jason didn't dare make him go any faster than a walk. Chafing at the delay, he forced himself to show Charity a patience he did not feel himself.

CHAPTER EIGHTEEN

Tippett awakened as the first gray of dawn touched the eastern horizon, and for reasons he could not explain, he immediately knew something was wrong. He seized his rifle, which he had laid close beside him, and leaped to his feet.

There was a lumped shape where Gruber had been. It occurred to him that Gruber might have faked that shape, so he stumbled to it and kicked it ungently with his toe. Gruber's grunt of protest sent a wave of relief through him. At least his prisoner had not escaped. Not that he'd have still been alive if Gruber had managed to free himself.

He glanced immediately toward the place where the two kids had been. They were no longer there. He rushed to where the horses had been picketed. Only two of them remained.

There could be no doubt as to where they had gone. To Denver, because he'd been fool enough to tell Jason yesterday that the two women had probably taken Matt there on the next regular stage. He should have kept his damn mouth shut.

But he discovered he not only didn't blame Jason for doing what he had done, he admired him. That was some kid, he thought.

He untied Gruber and told him to get up and get a fire built. While Gruber went after buffalo chips, he smashed the man's rifle against a rock. He stuck Gruber's revolver in the saddlebags along with the stolen money.

Gruber came back with a load of buffalo

159

chips. His scowl deepened when he saw the remains of his rifle, but he knelt and started a fire, growling, 'Where the hell did them kids disappear to?'

'Denver, I reckon. But they won't bother you no more, not where you're goin' to be.'

Gruber said, 'I ain't there yet.'

Tippett fried bacon and sliced some potatoes into the grease. When it was cooked, the two ate, finished the coffee, killed the fire, and saddled up. Tippett put his rope around the neck of Gruber's horse and tied the end fast to the horn of his own saddle. He rode out, maintaining a pace that kept the rope taut, not a hard thing to do, because Gruber's horse was tired.

Back along their trail they went, with Tippett wondering how long it would be before they would meet the others he had left following Gruber's trail.

It was midafternoon before he saw them coming toward him. When they met, the troopers looked at Gruber with intense relief. 'Get the money too?' asked Mott.

Tippett patted the saddlebags.

Mott asked, 'What happened to the kids?'

'They took out for Denver. I made the mistake of tellin' the boy that those two women had likely taken his brother with them day before yesterday.'

He handed the saddlebags to Mott. He handed the rope to another trooper and looked hopefully at the hostler who had been following the trail. 'Mind doing something for me?'

'What?'

'Asking Milton to drive that stage on to Denver so I can go after them two kids.'

'Hell, he ain't drove a stage for fifteen years.'

'It's somethin' a man don't forget.'

The man looked doubtful, but he nodded. 'All right.' He glanced at the other hostler. 'I guess we can take care of the place for a couple of days.'

Tippett nodded gratefully. He glanced at the trooper holding the rope around the neck of Gruber's horse. 'Watch him. He's slippery.'

The man said grimly, 'Don't worry. He killed Frank, and he ain't going to get away from me.'

Tippett watched them ride away, heading east toward the waystation on Coyote Creek. He himself turned west. By riding well into the night, he was able to reach his last night's camp a couple of hours after dark. At dawn of the following day he was following the trail of Jason's horse, all too aware that the boy was now twenty-four hours ahead of him.

*   *   *

Jason found out the first morning that the distance to the line of mountains was deceptive in the clear, high-plains air. Last night they had appeared to be no more than fifteen miles away, but by noon he had traveled fifteen miles and they still appeared to be just as far away.

The day was warm, the air fragrant with the coming of spring. Charity sat in front of him on the horse. He had a gun, and he knew Gruber was in custody. All he had to do was find Denver, and after that, find Matt.

He had no idea how big Denver was, and so had no idea how difficult would be his task. Following the precedent set down by Tippett, he halted often to rest and cool the horse's back. And he kept the animal at a walk.

The horse was beginning to limp slightly on the right forefoot, but an examination of it showed Jason nothing that might cause the limp. He supposed it could be a stone bruise on the frog. Or maybe the horse had simply been ridden too hard for too many days.

At dusk, he struck a road running north and south. Beyond the road he could see the shine of a river bordered on both sides by tall cottonwoods and thick underbrush. The river, he thought, must be the Platte. He knew Denver was on the Platte, but he had no way of knowing whether it was north or south.

He decided, since it was almost dark, that they'd camp near the road tonight. If any travelers came by, he could find out from them which direction the town of Denver was. He rode toward the river until he found a place where the grass was thick and long. Here he dismounted and lifted Charity down.

Both of them were dirty, and Charity's hair hadn't been combed for days. Jason picketed the horse and returned, using his last match to kindle a fire of dead cottonwood sticks.

He had taken some bacon and potatoes from Tippett's gunnysack. He put two potatoes into the fire to bake, and spitted the bacon on sticks. He had no canteen, so both he and Charity walked to the river bank to drink.

The fire had died to a bed of coals before Jason heard horses on the road. He immediately ran to it, and when two riders came along, waved both arms and yelled.

The riders stopped. One said, 'Hell, it ain't nothin' but a boy!'

The other asked, 'What's the matter, son?'

Jason didn't want to let them know that he and Charity were alone. He said, 'Pa told me to wait here by the road an' find out which way Denver was.'

'It's south. We're headed there.'

Jason asked, 'How far?'

'Fifteen, twenty miles maybe.'

Jason said, 'I'll tell him. Thanks.'

'Sure.' The two men rode on. Jason returned to Charity, who was nervously glancing around into the darkness. The bacon, spitted on the sticks, was done.

The two ate the potatoes, which were still hard, and the bacon, and went to the river again to drink. Then Jason got the blankets, and the two lay down to sleep. The fire died.

Jason found it hard to believe that they were free of Gruber. The man had been too persistent and too vicious for him to believe he had seen the last of him. He lay awake for a long time, worrying that Gruber might have gotten away from Tippett and followed them. Only by convincing himself it was ridiculous was he able finally to drop off to sleep.

It was dawn when he awoke. He got up, checked on the horse, then built up the fire. There was nothing to eat this morning, but he and Charity warmed themselves at the fire, drank some water from the river, then mounted and set out for Denver to search for Matt.

Once more Jason held the weary horse to a walk. In spite of that, the animal's limp became more pronounced. Finally both Jason and Charity dismounted and walked, leading the horse. It was late afternoon when they arrived.

On a rise to the north of town, Jason halted and stared unbelievingly. It was the largest city he had ever seen. There were literally hundreds of buildings and dozens of crisscrossing streets. There were buildings three stories high, built of brick. There were streetcars, drawn by horses, running back and forth along the streets.

And there was noise, the like of which Jason had never heard. Bells clanged. Men shouted. Dogs barked. Women screeched. The sound of iron tires on the cobblestone streets was a racket in itself, and there were heavy, iron-tired wagons everywhere. Oxen and cattle bawled.

The first thing Jason thought was: How are we ever going to find Matt? And indeed it appeared to be a formidable task. There must be many thousands of people in Denver, and there were thousands of houses, hotels, and roominghouses. People were coming and going all the time, by stagecoach, by buggy and freight wagon, by covered wagon, and by horseback.

As the two stared, the sun set behind the mountains in the west, the tops of which were still white with snow. Jason said impatiently, 'Well, come on. We ain't going to find Matt if we stand here gawking all night.'

Charity looked at him, her eyes trusting, and he knew she had no doubt about finding Matt. She had faith in him and trusted him.

But he had plenty of doubts about himself. He clenched his jaws angrily. He was the head of this family now, and doubts were something he could not afford. He'd find Matt, all right. He'd find him, no matter how difficult it might be.

But he was bleakly conscious that his pockets were empty, that they had no food, that they didn't even have a place to stay. He headed for the river bottom to camp. Tomorrow they'd begin their search for Matt. Once they had found him, they'd worry about how to get him away from the people who had taken him.

*   *   *

Gruber sat sullenly on his horse, scowling at the ground, neither looking at his captors nor speaking to them. His leg, though it seemed to be healing satisfactorily, still caused him considerable discomfort and pain.

Worse by far than the pain in his leg, though, was the bitter frustration that seethed endlessly in his mind. He'd had that money in his possession, that enormous quantity of money, and because he'd gotten overconfident, he'd let it be taken away from him. Worse, he was a prisoner, charged with two murders in addition to the theft. If he didn't escape, he was certain to be hanged.

But there was no use in trying to escape just yet. His horse was worn out. He had no food, and his rifle had been smashed, his revolver taken away from him.

No. Let them take him back to the waystation on Coyote Creek. Let them put him on the stage for Denver, and let them take him there. Then there would be plenty of time to think about escape. He'd never been to Denver, but he was willing to bet that their jail wasn't the most secure one in the world. He had been in lots of jails. There were always ways of breaking out.

He'd have to give up the idea of getting the

money back. That was impossible now. It was in the possession of the trooper Mott, and he wasn't likely to let it out of his sight. Furthermore, he'd be more than pleased if he got a chance to gun down the man who had killed his comrade Frank.

They traveled slowly so as to save the horses, and camped, and traveled again the day following, and camped again that night, and went on again. Gruber rode, glumly silent, planning, thinking about what he'd do when he managed to get free.

He'd find that goddamn kid, first of all. That Jason Huntzinger, who was the cause of every bad thing that had happened to him. When he did, he'd kill him with no more hesitation than he'd feel stepping on a bug, and with considerable more satisfaction. He didn't know about the girl. Maybe he'd kill her, and maybe he would not. But he promised himself Jason's death.

They reached the waystation finally. The hostlers hitched up the coach, and Milton mounted to the driver's box. Inside rode only Gruber and the fat man, Santistevan.

They rolled into Denver a week after Tippett had delivered Gruber into their custody. The three troopers took the money directly to the Clark Company and got a signed receipt for it. Then they delivered Gruber to the jail.

It was a damp, cold building with stone walls and a stone-block floor. At the windows there were thick steel bars. The cell doors had bars equally thick, and the jailer was a burly, sour-faced man who looked at Gruber as if he hated him.

CHAPTER NINETEEN

The first thing Jason did when he and Charity woke up was to take her to the river and make her wash. They had no comb, but he helped her straighten her hair by running his fingers through it like a comb. He cleaned himself up similarly.

Brushing their clothes helped very little, but they were clothes given them by the Indians, and their dirty condition wasn't as noticeable as if they had been made of cloth. He then boosted Charity up on the horse, mounted behind her, and rode up the small stream known as Cherry Creek to the town itself.

By making inquiries, he learned where the Overland Stage Depot was. He left Charity outside while he went in. It was much like the lobby of a hotel, with a desk at one side. He walked uncertainly to it and asked, 'The stagecoach from the east ... can you tell me if there was two women on it with a little boy?'

The man, wearing gold-rimmed glasses pinched to his nose, peered at him. 'Nope. Them two came in with some freight wagons.

168

Prim-lookin' young woman and one that was older. Boy was maybe four years old, I'd say. Sound like the ones you're lookin' for?'

'Yes, sir. Can you tell me where they went—which hotel, I mean?'

'Nope. Walked off up the street carryin' their own bags. Never seen 'em again.'

Jason nodded. He went out, and leading the horse with Charity still astride, walked up the street in the direction the stationmaster had indicated. He inquired at the first three hotels he came to, without success. It was like Jane Newton, Harriet Plowman, and Matt had vanished.

Charity's chin was quivering, and he scowled at her. She'd stood up under being kidnapped by Gruber and used as a hostage, but the thought of losing Matt was too much for her. Jason said, 'We just got to keep movin' around town. Sooner or later they got to bring him out.'

'What if he's already gone? There's people leavin' here all the time.'

'He ain't gone,' said Jason fiercely. 'He ain't gone, an' don't you say he is. We'll find him, but we got to keep lookin' until we do.'

'I'm hungry, Jason.'

'All right. I'll sell this here horse an' get us some food.' He turned in at the first livery stable. A little dried-up man with a week's untidy growth of whiskers on his face and a gamy smell asked, 'What ye want, boy?'

169

'I want to sell this horse.'

'Where'd ye get him?'

Jason said, 'He's mine. I got a right to sell him.'

'Got a bill of sale, have ye?'

'No, sir. But he's mine. I swear he is.'

'Can't buy no horses without a bill of sale. Want me to go to jail, do ye?'

'I'll give you a bill of sale.'

The man peered at the horse's hip, studying the brand. Finally the man said, 'Twenty dollars.'

Jason said angrily, 'That ain't enough, and you know it ain't. He's worth five or six times that much.'

'Not to me he ain't. Likely stolen, if ye ask me. Bill of sale or no bill of sale, I'm takin' a chance buyin' him at all.'

Jason said, 'Fifty.' He had to have more than twenty dollars. He had to have enough to get a place for them to live, to buy food enough to last until he could find some work.

'Twenty-five. Take it or leave it, boy. If you ain't takin' it, then get the hell out of here.'

'What about the saddle?'

'Five dollars, an' that's too much. But nobody ain't likely to be able to prove it's stolen like they can the horse.'

Jason knew when he was beat. He said, 'All right,' and lifted Charity down. The man gave him three ten-dollar gold pieces, and Jason and Charity walked out into the street. They found

170

a small restaurant run by an old Chinese man and his wife. Jason didn't figure the Chinese couple would wonder who they were and why they were alone. The food was good, and cheap, and they both ate all that they could hold.

Then they began walking up and down the streets, looking endlessly for Matt. Several times in the next several days they caught women watching them speculatively, and whenever they did, they ducked into the nearest alley and ran. But at the end of a week they still had not found Matt, and Jason was beginning to despair of ever finding him. He didn't tell Charity, but he was afraid Matt had been taken someplace else. By now he might be hundreds of miles away.

*   *   *

Gruber made himself a docile prisoner and forced himself to be cheerful with his jailer despite the bitter frustration that obsessed his mind.

When he was alone, he prowled back and forth, testing each bar, examining the walls, floor, and ceiling thoroughly. Satisfied that it was going to be impossible to break out, he began to make other plans.

At dusk the jailer brought Gruber's supper. He shoved the tray under the barred cell door. That eliminated any thought Gruber might have had about overcoming the jailer at mealtime. If the man wasn't going to unlock the door, there was no use thinking about overcoming him.

Frowning thoughtfully, Gruber ate the unpalatable, overcooked food. Finished, he put the tray on the floor beside his bunk.

The jailer came after it. He growled, 'Bring it over and shove it under the door.'

Gruber obeyed. He knew better than to refuse the jailer. Somehow he had to get the man to open the cell door and come inside, and it would serve no useful purpose to antagonize him.

The jailer turned down the lamp in the corridor. Gruber, the only prisoner in the jail, lay down on the cot to sleep.

The mattress was alive with bedbugs, but he was tired and almost immediately went to sleep. Light streaming through the jail window woke him. He got up and peered outside.

He had slept late. The sun was up. The jail window faced a street, and he could see people going past, wagons, and horsemen, sometimes a shining black, yellow-wheeled buggy.

The jailer brought his breakfast and shoved it beneath the door. Gruber, his leg stiff this morning, limped over to get it. He noticed the jailer looking at his wounded leg.

That gave him an idea. He picked up his breakfast, limped back, and sat down on the cot to eat. The jailer went away. Gruber's plan was simple, and its very simplicity might make it work. Every time the jailer saw him for the next couple of days, the limp was going to be worse, his pain from it increasingly noticeable on his face. Tomorrow he'd make the jailer believe the pain was nearly intolerable. He'd tell the man it was swollen up and red, and festering. That ought to force the jailer to fetch a doctor to look at it. When the doctor came into the cell, he'd seize him and make a hostage out of him. Forcing the doctor to accompany him, he'd make good his escape.

He made the limp a little worse, but not too much, when the jailer returned for the empty tray. He let his face show a slight grimace of pain with every movement that he made. The jailer disappeared and closed the door connecting the cells with the office out in front.

Gruber got up on his cot and stared out the barred window again. And suddenly he saw something that made his hands tighten fiercely on the bars, that made it even more urgent that he escape. He saw Jason Huntzinger walking down the street with his sister, Charity.

They were here! Those women must have brought the little boy to Denver with them, and Jason and his sister were hunting him. He could have his revenge against Jason, provided he could get out of this damned jail.

The pair disappeared. Gruber sat down on the cot to perfect his plans. He desperately wanted to hurry his escape, but he knew he ought to wait at least until tomorrow.

Each time the jailer came in today, he'd make his limp seem worse. By tomorrow, he would hardly be able to walk, and finally he would reluctantly admit to the jailer that his leg was killing him, that it was swollen up something terrible. He could fake the swelling by winding strips of blanket around his leg, then forcing his pants leg up over the wrapping so that it would be plainly tight. But he'd have to underplay his complaints, and he'd have to let calling a doctor be the jailer's idea instead of his. Any other course would raise the man's suspicions.

At noon the jailer brought his lunch. As usual, he pushed it underneath the door, but this time he waited, watching his prisoner.

Gruber got painfully to his feet. He hobbled toward the door with obvious difficulty. His face twisted. When he stooped to pick up the food, he nearly fell. The jailer watched but made no comment.

When the jailer returned for the tray, Gruber's progress to the door was even more painful than before. His pants leg seemed to be much too tight for his wounded leg. When he stooped to put down the tray, he nearly fell, catching himself barely in time by grabbing one of the bars and going to one knee. A groan of pain escaped his lips, as if wrenched from him.

He scowled angrily at the jailer. By an

174

apparently superhuman effort he pulled himself up with both hands on the bars. Turning his back on the jailer, he hobbled painfully to his cot.

He didn't look at the jailer again, but he could feel the man watching him. Finally the jailer left, and Gruber grinned triumphantly.

At dinner he repeated the performance, but this time it seemed even more difficult for him; it took longer, and his pants were even tighter around his wounded leg. The jailer asked sourly, 'That leg gettin' worse?'

Gruber only grunted. The jailer hesitated a moment, and finally he left.

In the morning, when the jailer brought his breakfast, Gruber couldn't stand. His pants were drum-tight on his wounded leg. He hopped to the cell door, his face contorted with the pain. Halfway there he fell. He landed on the wounded leg, and an involuntary yell of pain escaped his lips. His face broke out into a sweat.

He lay there, as if unconscious, for a couple of minutes, during which time the jailer stared at him with uncertainty and dismay. When the man finally hurried out, Gruber knew he had gone to send for a doctor. And he hadn't even had to ask. He should have been an actor on the stage, he thought.

After a while the jailer returned. When he heard the door, Gruber began to crawl painfully toward the cot. Reaching it, he put forth what seemed to be a superhuman effort to get himself up onto it. The jailer said, 'I got a doctor comin'. You shoulda told me that damn thing was gettin' worse. Now you're liable to lose the leg.'

Gruber only glared at him, his face still shiny with sweat.

The jailer said defensively, 'Don't you go blamin' me. It ain't my fault. I got no way of knowin' how your goddamn leg feels.'

Gruber still did not speak. He continued to glare at the man. The jailer turned and went back to the office to await the doctor's arrival.

Trying hard to stifle his triumphant glee, Gruber waited. Falling on the leg had brought real pain and had succeeded in making sweat spring out on his face. It had fooled the jailer, and it ought to fool the doctor, at least until he was inside the cell.

He heard the outside door, the murmur of voices, and finally the inside door. A middle-aged man in a business suit came in, carrying a bag. The jailer unlocked the cell, and the doctor came inside.

Gruber moved like a panther. He was up off the cot in an instant. He seized the doctor around the neck, choking him so that he couldn't breathe. At the jailer he snarled, 'Back off, or you got a dead doc on your hands.' As he spoke, he moved swiftly toward the open door of the cell.

The jailer drew his gun. Gruber said,

'Drop it!'

The doctor's face was purple now. His eyes rolled with helpless terror at the jailer. The jailer hesitated only an instant. Then he dropped the gun.

Gruber shoved the doctor at the jailer violently. The two collided and went down in a heap. Gruber picked up the gun. He snapped, 'In the cell, both of you!'

Jailer and doctor, thoroughly terrified, scurried into the cell. Gruber said, 'Down on the floor, both of you!'

The men lay down, their terror plain in their eyes. They were both certain they were going to be murdered.

Gruber stooped. He struck twice quickly with the gun barrel, leaving both men bleeding and limp on the stone-block floor.

Gruber went into the jail office. He selected a rifle from the rack, got cartridges for it and for the revolver. Then he stepped out into the street. None of the busy passersby even looked at him.

CHAPTER TWENTY

Jason Huntzinger had dug a cave in a clay bank overlooking the swift-flowing Platte. Working with only a sharp-edged stone, he had hollowed it out so that it was large enough to

177

hold them both, deep enough to hide them from the sight of anyone passing by unless they happened to be close and looking straight into it.

All day, every day for the last week, they had walked the Denver streets, looking either for Matt or for the women who had brought him here. They'd had no success.

On the morning of Gruber's escape they left the cave at sunup as usual. They walked to the river bank and washed, something Charity would have forgone but for Jason's insistence on it. Jason knew, if she did not, that the more unkempt they were, the more likely it was that they'd be taken for orphans by well-meaning women of the town.

As usual, they ate at the Chinese restaurant, and afterward went out into the bright, warm sunlight to begin their search of the Denver streets.

They saw Matt at almost the same instant that Gruber spotted them. Skulking in an alley, he saw them pass, and they might have seen him too except that both of them were looking at Matt, seated between Mrs Plowman and her husband in a shiny passing buggy.

Jason shouted, 'Matt!' and young Matt turned his head to look. He tried to crawl over Mrs Plowman and jump out of the buggy, but she held him tightly, while her husband whipped the buggy horse and forced him into a trot.

Jason and Charity broke into a run. Gruber broke out of the alley and ran after them. Jason shouted helplessly, 'Matt! Matt!' and then stopped shouting to save his breath for the pursuit.

The buggy drew steadily away. Jason, panting and out of breath, knew it was going to get away. Without a horse he didn't have a chance of catching it.

He stopped, fuming helplessly. Charity had lagged behind, and he turned his head to see where she was. It was then that he saw Gruber, running toward them and no more than fifty feet away.

He bawled, 'Charity!' and saw her glance around. Seeing Gruber gave her the incentive she needed to forget how out of breath she was. She darted toward Jason, and he ducked into a passageway between two buildings, with Charity close on his heels. At the end of the passageway he moved aside and slowed slightly to let her go ahead. He didn't know how Gruber had gotten loose, whether he'd killed Tippett and escaped or whether he'd escaped from the Denver jail, and it didn't matter anyway. But he did know one thing: if he and Charity stayed together, they were going to be caught. Charity simply could not run fast enough to stay out of Gruber's reach. And if she was caught, he would have to give himself up to save her life.

He yelled. 'Go back to the cave!' and when

179

she glanced back at him in terror, he shouted harshly, 'Damnit, for once you do what I say!'

He didn't wait to see what she would do. He only knew Gruber couldn't chase them both. He also knew Gruber wanted him more than he wanted Charity. He made a sharp right turn and ran along the alley, trying to breathe deeply and slowly, knowing full well that right now he was literally running for his life.

Gruber was still trying to catch him, because he didn't want to attract attention by firing his gun. But the minute Gruber thought he was going to get away, he'd stop, take careful aim, and shoot Jason down.

Jason suddenly knew how a rabbit felt when it was being chased by a dog. He left the alley, after spotting another passageway between two tall brick buildings. He raced toward its entrance.

A large wooden packing case stood just beside the opening. As Jason passed it, he seized it and dragged it after him into the passageway. Glancing over it, he saw Gruber just entering the passageway less than twenty feet away.

Gruber could have killed him easily, but he still was apparently afraid of attracting attention with a gunshot. He raced toward the packing case, tried to jump over it, and failed. Jason was out into the street then, leaving Gruber wrestling with the packing case. He finally lifted it and carried it forward along the passageway to its end. By the time Gruber burst into the street and flung the packing case disgustedly aside, Jason was half a block away.

Gruber pounded after him, now shouting excitedly, 'Stop, thief! Stop that boy!'

Someone stuck out a foot, and Jason sprawled headlong. Hands clutched at him, but he squirmed away and darted once more down a passageway between two buildings. He knew, then, that he'd have to stay out of crowds even if it did expose him to the fire from Gruber's gun. But he couldn't run much longer. If he didn't get away in the next couple of blocks, he was going to get caught. And if he got caught, he was going to get killed.

Tippett didn't know that Gruber had escaped. He had talked to Mary about taking the three children, and she had agreed, provided she got to meet them first. Now the two of them were driving up and down the busy Denver streets looking for Jason and Charity, who, Tippett guessed, would probably also be prowling the streets looking for their brother, Matt.

Tippett heard the shout, 'Stop thief! Stop that boy!' and turned his head to look. He saw Jason tripped, saw him sprawl headlong, saw him squirm away and dart into a passageway. He saw Gruber disappear into the passageway after him.

He handed the reins to his wife, leaped from the buckboard seat, and ran. He had the

181

advantage of being fresh, and almost immediately began to gain.

Gruber now carried his rifle in both hands, across his chest, so that he could bring it up and fire it instantly. Tippett had only his revolver, in its holster at his side, and he didn't dare fire at Gruber because of the boy running ahead of him.

Along the alley they went, burst into a street, crossed it, and entered the alleyway beyond. Jason was plainly tiring, and Gruber was gaining on him. But Tippett was also gaining on Gruber, who still did not know he was being pursued.

Halfway along the second block, Jason glanced behind. He saw how close Gruber was, but he also saw Tippett racing along behind.

He stopped suddenly. Triumphantly, Gruber raced toward him. Nearing him, Gruber raised his rifle, plainly intending to strike the boy with it.

Tippett skidded to a halt. He yanked his revolver from its holster and thumbed the hammer back. He raised it, leveled it. He was going to have to chance a shot; he was going to have to risk hitting the boy. If he did not, Jason was going to be killed.

Gruber was now less than ten feet from the exhausted boy. But suddenly Jason came to life. He straightened, and putting forth one last violent burst of energy, he dived through an opening in a board fence and disappeared.

182

Gruber skidded to a halt. He stooped to go through the opening in pursuit. Tippett stopped him with his roar, 'Gruber! Hold it right where you are!'

Gruber spun around. His rifle was in both hands, held at the ready across his chest. The distance between Tippett and himself was a little long for a short-barreled revolver, and perhaps that was why he took the chance. He flung the rifle to his shoulder, took aim at Tippett, and fired.

Tippett's bullet left his gun a split-second before smoke blossomed from the muzzle of Gruber's rifle. He knew, even as he fired, that Gruber's chance of hitting him was at least twice as good as his chance of hitting Gruber.

Gruber's rifle slug tore into the muscles of Tippett's thigh and dumped him into the alley dust. There was no pain. There was only a numbing shock and surprise to find himself sprawled out on the ground. He fought to bring the revolver to bear again.

Lying flat, with the gun steadied in both hands held out in front of him, he took aim at Gruber a second time.

Gruber was faster a second time because of the fact that he was on his feet. The rifle was steadied, aimed straight at Tippett, and in an instant it would fire, and this time Tippett knew he would be dead.

Before the rifle could fire, Jason dived from behind the fence. As he did, Tippett fired,

183

unable to hold back his shot. Gruber also fired, but Jason's body struck his legs just as he did. The bullet went skyward, striking a brick wall and ricocheting away.

Tippett's bullet didn't miss. It took Gruber squarely in the chest. Like a powerful blow, it flung him back. He sprawled in the alley dust, dead before he hit the ground.

Jason got slowly to his feet and stood rooted, as if stunned. For a moment Tippett thought he was going to run away. Tippett struggled to one knee, trying to make it to his feet. His thigh was burning like fire now, and his pants were soaked with blood.

Jason hesitated uncertainly. The boy had saved his life, Tippett thought, and he wondered what Jason was going to do now.

The boy had little reason to trust anyone, he thought, except perhaps an Indian. He was fighting desperately to keep his family together, and everybody seemed to be trying to split them up. But Tippett didn't say anything. He just waited, looking at Jason, trying not to let the pain he was feeling show on his face.

Jason's glance went to Tippett's bloody leg. And suddenly he made up his mind. He came to Tippett and said, 'You can lean on me.'

Tippett, with Jason supporting him, struggled to his feet. There were people coming along the alley now, and behind them the buckboard with Mary Tippett holding the reins.

184

Tippett looked down into Jason's dirty face. He said, 'That's Mrs Tippett, son. We'd be proud to have you and Charity and Matt stay with us until something better comes along.'

Some of the tension seemed to go out of the boy's scared and worried face. Tippett said, 'Come on. I reckon I'd better get someplace and have this leg tied up.'

Jason, as serious about this as about everything he did, helped him hobble along the alley toward the waiting buckboard and the pleasant-faced but frightened woman sitting on the seat.

Lewis B. Patten wrote more than ninety Western novels in thirty years and three of them won Golden Spur Awards from the Western Writers of America and the author himself the Golden Saddleman Award. Indeed, this points up the most remarkable aspect of his work: not that there is so much of it, but that so much of it is so fine. Patten was born in Denver, Colorado, and served in the U.S. Navy 1933-1937. He was educated at the University of Denver during the war years and became an auditor for the Colorado Department of Revenue during the 1940s. It was in this period that he began contributing significantly to Western pulp magazines, fiction that was from the beginning fresh and unique and revealed Patten's lifelong concern with the sociological and psychological affects of group psychology on the frontier. He became a professional writer at the time of his first novel, MASSACRE AT WHITE RIVER (1952). The dominant theme in much of his fiction is the notion of justice, and its opposite, injustice. In his first novel it has to do with exploitation of the Ute Indians, but as he matured as a writer he explored this theme with significant and poignant detail in small towns throughout the early West. Crimes, such as rape or lynching, were often at the center of his stories. When the values embodied in these small towns are examined closely, they are found to be wanting. Conformity is always easier than taking a stand. Yet, in Patten's view of the American West, there is usually a man or a woman who refuses to conform. Among his finest titles, always a difficult choice, surely are A KILLING AT KIOWA (1972), RIDE A CROOKED TRAIL (1976), and his many fine contributions to Doubleday's Double D series, including VILLA'S RIFLES (1977), THE LAW AT COTTONWOOD (1978), and DEATH RIDES A BLACK HORSE (1978). His most recent books are TINCUP IN THE STORM COUNTRY and TRAIL TO VICKSBURG, both published as Five Star Westerns.

We hope you have enjoyed this Large Print book. Other Chivers Press or G.K. Hall & Co. Large Print books are available at your library or directly from the publishers.

For more information about current and forthcoming titles, please call or write, without obligation, to:

Chivers Press Limited
Windsor Bridge Road
Bath BA2 3AX
England
Tel. (01225) 335336

OR

G.K. Hall & Co.
P.O. Box 159
Thorndike, Maine 04986
USA
Tel. (800) 223–2336

All our Large Print titles are designed for easy reading, and all our books are made to last.